A CORPSE AT THE COVE

SUNRISE ISLAND MYSTERIES, BOOK 3

BLYTHE BAKER

❀ Created with Vellum

~

At the quaint little Sunrise Island Bed & Breakfast, guests check in ... and never check out.

Piper Lane's seaside bed & breakfast is finally up and running. What's more, new romances are blooming in the lives of all three Lane women. Life on the sunny island can't get any better. There's just one problem – and it's a corpse.

When a disgruntled guest meets a violent end and someone close to home becomes a suspect, Piper puts on her detective hat once again. But can she catch a killer before more unlucky guests become permanent residents?

~

CHAPTER 1

I delicately lifted a white porcelain lamp into the air, checking the underside for a price tag. Why anyone would place a price tag on the bottom of a breakable item was beyond me. Though, on second thought, the store was wallpapered with 'YOU BREAK IT, YOU BUY IT' signs, so perhaps the owner had the right idea. Make every customer hold a fragile lamp above their head before they can buy it and someone is bound to drop one.

Eighty dollars!

Just as delicately, I returned the lamp to its perch on a rickety wooden credenza and continued my perilous journey through the store. The aisles were narrow, especially considering the ever-increasing size of the average Texan. Again, I had to wonder whether the owner wasn't banking on a few plump rumps knocking into the priceless knick-knacks balanced on the edges of bookcases and end tables. 'YOU BREAK IT, YOU BUY IT.'

The store was a bit out of my price range—some of the antique tables were worth more than I made in a month at my old bank job—but I was growing desperate. I'd scoured every estate sale, junk shop, and antique store on Sunrise Island until I finally gave up, hopped on a ferry, and tried my luck on the mainland. It was the first time I'd left the island in three months.

Every spare second for months had been spent on renovating the old bed and breakfast, and now that Sunrise B&B was officially up and running and accepting guests, I had more time than I'd imagined on my hands. While I'd headed up most of the renovations, my sister Page was taking full charge of making sure the guests felt welcomed. Perhaps it had something to do with the fact that the first guest I'd checked in had never checked out.

Holly Belden's death made headlines everywhere, due in part to her having worked as a reporter for a rather large newspaper. Her colleagues honored her memory with front page spreads for the better part of a week. Though, the case was also rather sensational. Guests trapped in a mansion during a storm, being picked off one by one by a deranged killer. It sounded more like a summer blockbuster than anything that could happen on a tiny island south of Houston, and the people were curious.

Luckily, Holly's connection to the bed and breakfast was far from the main focus of the story, and my name managed to stay out of the papers because Sheriff Shepherd didn't want to admit that I'd solved yet another murder case before he was able to. All of which was perfectly fine with me. I wanted to be remembered for my entrepreneurial skills, and maybe my banana pancakes, not my penchant for foiling the plans of serial killers.

Also, by some miracle, very few of the bed and breakfast's first guests knew anything about the killer who had lived next door, and those that did know about Martin Little had no idea that I'd been the one to discover his secret and kill him when he tried to attack me. Page had explained to her daughter in no uncertain terms that she was not allowed to use the story of her serial killer-fighting aunt as an ice breaker at her new school. Miraculously, the deaths that had occurred on the bed and breakfast property had stayed under wraps, and the last thing we needed were a bunch of high school students going home and sharing the news with their parents. Weekenders from Houston who were popping down to the island for a "staycation" of sorts were our bread and butter. We couldn't risk losing their business.

And according to Page, part of keeping our customers happy and returning was personalizing the rooms so they didn't feel like a cookie cutter hotel room. We needed more "character," Page said, so I'd been designated the interior decorator. The tastemaker, if you will. My first decision as the decorator was to avoid all of the shops along the beach on the mainland. They were mainly stocked with "Life is a Beach" signs and lamps covered in seashells, and 'tourist destination' was not the vibe I wanted the Sunrise B&B to give off. We wanted to feel authentic, one of a kind. So, I'd steered away from the pleasure pier and its carnival atmosphere in favor of the inland antique and junk shops downtown. I'd also brought my niece Blaire with me. If anyone could spot cheesy, it was Blaire. She had a rather strong opinion about most things and wasn't afraid to voice it.

"What do you think of this, Blaire?" I asked over my shoulder, holding up a wrought iron bookend in the shape of a bike tire. The bed and breakfast had beautiful built-in bookshelves, and we were currently working on expanding our library beyond Page's romance novels and my excessive collection of unopened cookbooks.

When Blaire didn't answer immediately, I turned around, expecting to find her staring at me, one eyebrow raised, sporting an expression that said, *You can't be serious, Aunt Piper.* Instead, I turned to find no one behind me except the ancient shop owner who was paying me zero attention, instead squinting towards the miniscule cube television she had sitting on the counter. I couldn't tell what she was watching, but I imagined it was either a game show or a talk show.

"Blaire?" I called, slipping down the aisles looking for her. She couldn't have gone far because she was holding onto Jasper, my French Bulldog. He'd been on his leash, but I'd instructed Blaire to hold him in her arms while we were in the shops, lest his curiosity got the best of him and he knocked over an entire display of antique salt and pepper shakers. 'YOU BREAK IT, YOU BUY IT.'

Perhaps she went outside so she could set him back on the ground, I thought.

I made it to the front door without breaking anything, waved to the old woman behind the counter, and stepped outside into the tail end of a south Texas summer. There was a slight breeze coming from the ocean a few blocks away, but otherwise the day was humid and sticky. My cardigan suddenly felt too heavy, and I pulled it off and tied it around my waist, knowing I looked like a suburban mom at a theme park. Nevertheless, I was too concerned to care. I squinted against the sun and scanned up and down the block, seeing no sign of Blaire or Jasper.

Blaire was sixteen, and very capable of taking care of herself, but that didn't stop my heart from lurching in my chest as I pulled out my phone and punched in her number. It rang what felt like one thousand times before her deadpan voice instructed me to leave a message after the beep. I barked into the phone for her to call me back immediately, turned my ringer volume to high so I wouldn't miss her call, and took off down the block.

Normally I wouldn't have been near as paranoid, but something about running across two murderers in the span of three months had set me on edge. Certainly, I'd reached my lifetime quota of crazy, right? I wanted to think so, but there was no guarantee. Had Blaire been targeted by someone? She was a pretty girl, after all. Had she trusted the wrong person and ended up in the back of a windowless white van? Gruesome thoughts flashed through my mind, though I was trying hard to squash them.

I passed a coffee shop, and pressed my face to the window, ignoring the awkward stares from a young couple sipping their coffees and splitting what looked like a blueberry muffin. Blaire wasn't inside, so I moved on. As

I came to the end of the block, I noticed a barely there tattoo shop across the street shoved between a travel agent office and an antique shop we'd already been in. The shop had a bizarrely narrow focus on animal-print antiques, and Blaire and I had spent less than a minute inside before deciding we needed to get out before the owner nabbed Jasper and turned him into a foot stool. Had she noticed the tattoo parlor when they were there earlier and gone back, unable to resist the lure of teenage rebellion? I found myself both hoping she was inside and desperately hoping she was anywhere else. I couldn't decide whether it would be worse to return home without Blaire or to return her to her mother covered in tattoos and body piercings.

I jogged across the street, ignoring the signs that forbade jaywalking, and ducked into the dimly lit shop. Neon signs cluttered the walls, advertising 'walk-ins welcome' and 'nose piercings.' I sent up a prayer that I wasn't too late.

"Can I help you?" a woman with spiky pink hair and too many piercings to count asked.

Despite her aesthetic, she had a warm, open face, and a blindingly white smile.

"I'm looking for my niece," I said, my statement turning up at the end in a kind of half question.

The woman gestured both arms to the shop around her as if to say, "Ta-da!"

"This is all there is," she said.

One quick look around the teeny space told me Blaire wasn't there. I thanked the woman for her time and turned to leave.

"Can I interest you in anything while you're here?" she asked. "Half-off your first piercing."

I looked back, trying to decide if she was joking or not, and upon deciding that she was entirely serious, I said, "No thanks. I'm going to make sure my niece hasn't been kidnapped before I permanently alter my body."

The woman nodded her pink head and turned away, clearly not concerned with my plight.

I stepped back onto the bright street and checked my phone to make sure Blaire hadn't called. Nothing.

"Crap, crap, crap," I muttered under my breath.

Then, I noticed a shop further down the block, a glowing neon hand hanging from the door advertising psychic readings and crystals. I suddenly remembered Blaire saying something about the healing power of crystals a few weeks back, and beelined for the shop.

As soon as I'd opened the door, my eyes began to water. The smell of herbs and incense was powerful, and it felt like someone had stuffed sandalwood down my throat and directly into my lungs. Fighting against the urge to close the door and take deep, slow breaths of the fresh air outside, I walked into the shop, the bell above the door ringing at my arrival.

Immediately, a small, modest woman draped in a purple sash stepped from the back of the shop and smiled at me as though we were old friends.

"Welcome," she said. "How can I assist you today?"

"I'm actually just looking for my niece," I said. "Medium height, dark black hair, hopefully in the company of a particularly hyper dog."

The woman laughed a dry laugh, like autumn leaves

rubbing together in the wind. "Yes, yes. I have what you seek."

She disappeared behind the curtain, and I stood in the doorway for a few seconds, unsure if I should follow her. When she said she had what I sought, did she mean that she had Blaire behind that curtain or, in typical phony psychic fashion, that she had the information of where Blaire was? Or was it more sinister than even that? If I went behind the curtain, would I find Blaire and Jasper tied up in her back room? Was she going to grind down our bones for some kind of voodoo magic?

Taking a deep breath, I tried to convince myself I was being ridiculous, and I moved through the shop, passing glass cases of different colored crystals, countless sticks of incense, and several shelves of books about homeopathic medicine.

If I thought the front of the shop smelled, it was nothing compared to the back. Mixing with the over-bearing scent of incense was an even stronger smell of dust and mildew. Dark blue curtains hung from the ceiling, tied back with silver tassels, giving the room the appearance of a tent. The drapes completely blocked all of the air vents, making the room little more than a heat box. My lungs tightened, and I struggled to take in air.

"Hey, Aunt Piper," Blaire said.

I turned to see her sitting behind a round table, her hand lying flat and open on the table, Jasper sitting at her feet, his tongue lolling from the side of his mouth.

"*Hey Aunt Piper,*" I repeated, my voice high and mocking. "You didn't think it was worth mentioning to me where you were going? I've been searching everywhere for you."

Her face paled only slightly. "Sorry. I didn't think I'd be gone long. Jasper needed to go to the bathroom, and then I came across the street to throw away his poo bag, and I saw the crystal shop. I was just going to duck inside for a second, but then Cibil offered me a free palm reading."

I turned back to the small woman who was taking her seat across from Blaire, her fingers running over the lines of Blaire's hand. She looked over her shoulder at me, a vacant smile dancing across her lips.

"I'll give you one, too," she said before turning her attention back to Blaire. "For your trouble."

"No, really, I'm fine," I said. "Besides, Blaire and I should be going."

Cibil shook her head. "Not so much rushing. Blaire needs to slow down."

Blaire's eyes widened and she looked over at me, panicked.

"What do you mean 'slow down'?" I asked, hating myself for being curious.

Cibil winked at Blaire, and patted her palm reassuringly. "It is not for anyone but Blaire to know."

Blaire's clear relief made me that much more curious.

"You should get a reading, Aunt Piper," Blaire said as she stood up, Jasper stirring, but looking too lazy to stand.

I used to be rather superstitious, even checking my horoscope to see what I should expect from my month. However, then I went on a blind date with a guy who told me he wrote horoscopes for a local magazine. The date was a disaster, and I decided he was the last person I wanted having any kind of influence on my life, so I gave up the habit. I didn't know much about Cibil, but I also didn't care to have her input on my life. Nevertheless, almost as if by some outside force, I found myself crossing the room and lowering into the plush velvet chair across from her.

She reached across the table and grabbed my hand before I had time to second guess myself. She laid my hand palm up on the table and her fingers began probing the deep and delicate lines of my hand, moving over my skin as lightly as a spider, her eyes closed in concentration. Then, almost as quickly as it had begun, she pulled her hands back, opened her eyes, and looked at me, sadness welling in them.

"What is it?" I finally asked, too anxious to wait for her to decide to speak.

She took a deep breath. "There is blood on your hands."

The image of Martin Little, limp and lifeless in the hole he'd intended to act as my unmarked grave flashed in my mind, but I said nothing.

"She killed a man," Blaire said, practically bursting with the information.

I whipped my head towards her, my eyes blazing a warning.

"A man attacked her and she fought him off," she clarified, shrugging in apology.

Cibil shook her head. "It is not the past I see, but the future."

The woman stared into my eyes, as though she were

looking directly into my soul, and I pulled away from her gaze, feeling uncomfortable.

"Great," I said, standing up, prodding Jasper with my foot until he groggily rose to his feet and moved towards the exit. "Thanks for the warning."

"Will she uncover another murderer?" Blaire asked, enraptured. "She has already caught two."

I moved towards my niece and wrapped an arm around her, squeezing her shoulders as tightly as I could. She winced and moved out of my grip.

Cibil narrowed her eyes. "That has yet to be determined. Violence will find you again, though. This time, striking much closer to home."

I let out a bark-like laugh, making Jasper jump. Cibil and Blaire both turned to me, confused looks on their faces.

"My next-door neighbor was a murderer and a dead body turned up on our property. How much closer to home could danger be?" I asked, half-laughing, turning to Blaire.

She looked concerned. Cibil's expression once again looked apologetic, and suddenly I didn't find the prediction so funny. A chill ran down my spine.

"Come on, Blaire," I said, grabbing her shoulder and turning her towards the door. "It's time to go."

We moved quickly through the shop, and I glanced behind me one last time before stepping out onto the street. The woman had followed us only as far as the doorway that led to the back where her palm reading table was set up. She was leaning against the frame, her purple shawl pulled tightly around her despite the almost unbearable warmth of the room. She lifted one hand in a wave, and I couldn't help but feel she was saying something much more than goodbye.

I tossed a wave over my shoulder and let the door bang closed behind me, the daylight almost immediately ridding me of any worries about the woman's prediction.

CHAPTER 2

We grabbed cheeseburgers from a diner by the beach, and ate them as we walked to the ferry. I knew Page would never approve of greasy red meat as dinner, but what she didn't know wouldn't hurt her. I didn't become the favorite aunt by listening to all of Page's rules, after all. Besides, I knew Blaire would never tell.

Blaire groaned as she chewed a huge mouthful of her burger. "This is so much better than mom's turkey burgers. I mean, her turkey burgers are pretty good. But this," she pointed to the wrapper in her hand, grease dripping down the paper and falling to the ground, "this is way better."

I nodded in agreement. "One of the hard truths of life is that the things that taste best are usually terrible for you. I mean, think about it. Does anyone actually claim their favorite food is carrot sticks or spinach? No. It's cheesecake and fried chicken and pizza."

I ripped off a chunk of my burger and dropped it on

the ground for Jasper. He launched himself at it, practically falling over as he clamped his jaws over the patty and swallowed it whole.

"I know that," Blaire said. "It's why mom implements a cheat meal every week."

My head snapped towards her hard enough that I tweaked a muscle in my neck. "A cheat meal? No, she doesn't."

For as long as I could remember, Page had been a health nut. Even when we were teenagers, she ate half a grapefruit and bran cereal for breakfast while berating me for my colorful, sugary cereal of choice. She was normally done with yoga for twenty minutes and was sitting at the kitchen table drinking a weird mixture of Apple Cider Vinegar and lemon juice when I finally stumbled out of bed and groggily went to the kitchen to make my first cup of coffee.

Blaire smiled, her eyes lit up and amused. "I saw her eat THREE milk chocolate bars last week. For breakfast."

My mouth fell open. "Fun-size or regular size?"

If it was possible, Blaire's smile grew even wider. "King."

"King size?" I balked, shaking my head, hardly able to believe it. "I would have paid money to see that."

"Just 'accidentally' walk in the bathroom after she claims she is going to 'soak in the tub,' and you can see it for free. She hides a cheese can behind the guest towels."

I took another bite of my burger and shook my head. "You are wise beyond your years, Blaire."

She shrugged. "At least when it comes to my mom. I

figured it out when I was only ten years old, but she managed to keep it a secret from dad."

Our conversation dropped into a companionable silence, and the sun setting over the ocean cast the world in shades of oranges and pinks, making for the perfect sherbet afternoon.

The sun was sinking quickly behind the horizon, and the ferry ride was quieter than normal, filled with work weary commuters who had office jobs in the city, but lived on Sunrise Island. Though we'd been on the island for three months already, this was only the third time I'd ridden the ferry to or from the island. The air felt so much cooler than it did on land. Even sitting on the beach was nothing compared to the brisk breeze whipping over the ocean.

Besides, I had rather lost my taste for the beach. Something about finding a dead body buried in the sand really ruins your appetite for sun tanning. Nathaniel Sharpe's murder would have been nothing more than a local curiosity to me had he not been buried on the private beach that had come with my purchase of the bed and breakfast. My discovery of his body had set me on a course that I'd never imagined taking—searching for clues, following up on leads, and, ultimately, solving the case. Not to mention, nearly getting myself murdered in the process.

Martin Little was just as much, if not more, to blame for my sudden disinterest in beaches as Nathaniel Sharpe.

Especially since Martin Little was the one who buried Nathaniel Sharpe on my beach, and then tried to bury me when I discovered his secret. The whole debacle still felt too bizarre to be real. Surely I, the previous bank teller who was dumped by her boyfriend and fired on the same day—oh, did I forget to mention that my boss was my boyfriend?—couldn't possibly be an amateur sleuth. Nevertheless, it seemed that was what I'd become.

After solving Nathaniel Sharpe's murder, I'd then gone on to attend the fateful dinner party that saw the bed and breakfast's first guest, Holly Belden, murdered along with the party's host, Robert Baines. Trapped in Robert Baines's mansion due to a tropical storm the island was still recovering from, I'd followed a few hunches and discovered Jimmy, owner of the only decent restaurant on Sunrise Island, had killed them both. Not only had dinner parties been suddenly added to the list—just after beaches —of places I no longer cared to frequent, but Jimmy's restaurant closed its doors for good. Of course, I was glad Jimmy's Daily Catch had closed because it meant Jimmy was behind bars where he belonged. The trouble was that I now had nowhere to order seafood I could guarantee wouldn't give me food poisoning. The general store's pre-packaged, refrigerated sushi was definitely not an option, though I had caught myself eyeing it a bit more frequently.

Plus, if the island lost any more businesses, there was a risk that the tourist crowd would dry up. Sure, most people came to the island for a fun day at the beach, but there had to be other things for them to do, too, especially if we wanted them to stay overnight at the Sunrise Bed and Breakfast. Which we decidedly did, considering Page and I had both poured all our savings into renovating the large Victorian house. If the business failed, we had no back up plan. Page had just finalized the sale on the house she'd shared with her (now) ex-husband in Houston, and I had bailed out of my apartment's lease six months early to move to the island. The early cancellation fees alone had been a deep cut into my savings account. So, seeing Sunrise Island's murder rate skyrocket and the best restaurant on Main Street close hadn't exactly left us feeling super confident. Though, I tried to remind myself that we had a house full of guests, and were booked through the rest of the summer.

The island came into view on the horizon, the pastel-colored houses along the beach standing high on stilts to avoid high tide and flooding, looking like a picture-perfect postcard you'd find in a rack at the gift shop. The kind of image you'd see and say, "Yeah right, that place couldn't possibly exist."

The first time I'd seen the island, I'd been drawn in by the sapphire blue water lapping against the sand, the beach houses nestled amongst the palm trees. On the mainland, palm trees felt artificial to me. Like a kind of tourist trap. They were planted everywhere—outside of banks, in the medians of the roads, all through my old apartment complex. It felt as if I was being manipulated into believing that, even though the nearest beach was at least a forty-five-minute drive, I'd been blessed to live in a tropical paradise. On the island, though, the palm trees looked natural.

I also remembered being surprised by the empty

beach. Beaches on the mainland were almost always crowded with people—moms smearing sun cream on their screaming children, couples holding hands, college kids throwing frisbees and drinking beer from red solo cups like they were in a spring break movie. Of course, now I knew that the first time I'd seen the island, it had simply been too early for tourists. The ferry only carried people to and from the island twice a day, once in the early morning and once in the late afternoon. Visitors to the island disembarked on the early ferry, sun hats and fanny packs in tow, and began filling the beaches by mid-morning. That was another reason the Bed and Breakfast had been doing so well. People were willing to pay for a night at the B&B to ensure they had access to our private beach, one of the few stretches of sand that wasn't clogged with people by 2 PM. Apparently, whether a body had been found in the sand was a minor concern.

"Do you see anything, Aunt Piper?"

Blaire's voice drew me out of my thoughts and I turned to her, eyes wide and confused.

She gestured to the beach, leaning forward to rest her elbows on the railing, her brow furrowing as she looked over the water. "You know, like a body or a clue? Or is it more of a tingling feeling you get, like a sixth sense?"

I stared at her, hoping she could feel my icy glare reaching deep down into her soul. Blaire, as impervious as always, didn't seem too affected, though. She continued staring at me, actually waiting for me to respond to her ridiculous question.

"There aren't going to be any more murders," I said with finality, reaching down to pet the top of Jasper's head, scratching the extra fluffy spot behind his ear. "And even if there were, I wouldn't be able to *sense* them. I haven't come into contact with any radioactive material or been sent here from another planet. This isn't a comic book. It's real life, and real people died."

"Oh, relax," she said. "I'm only kidding about the extra sense thing. But you should be on the lookout for anything suspicious. You heard what Cibil said."

I turned to face her, trying to make sure she heard me and that my words wouldn't be misunderstood. "That woman was a joke. Her predictions were vague and nondescript. People like her say things like that so that when you're rushing down the stairs and you trip and fall, you can remember she told you not to hurry. Or when a poisonous snake turns up in the backyard, I'll remember that she told me danger was lurking nearby. It's a ploy to bring back customers and steal their money. She has to give everyone a prediction, otherwise she doesn't get paid."

"We didn't pay her," Blaire said, not addressing anything else I'd said. "She gave us our palm readings for free. That doesn't exactly sound like some money hungry fake to me."

"Are you honestly saying you believe what that woman said?" I asked.

Blaire shrugged.

I shook my head and turned back to the ocean. Sunrise Island was so close now I could make out several clusters of picnicking families on the beach, lounging on beach towels while they ate their sandwiches.

"Don't mention any of this to your mom," I said,

thinking about Page's strong aversion to anything even slightly mystical. "The last thing I need is for her to hear that I not only let you wander around the city by yourself, but that you were also manipulated by some nut job with a crystal ball."

"She didn't have a crystal ball," Blaire muttered, but she nodded in agreement when I fixed her with a stare.

The speakers on deck sputtered to life, and through the thick static we heard, "Welcome to Sunrise Island."

Despite my insistence that Cibil's prediction had been a hoax, I found myself scanning the beach one last time, looking for anything even remotely out of place.

CHAPTER 3

Mason was waiting for us, leaning against the driver's side door of his blue sedan. I'd almost forgotten he'd promised to pick us up, and I was relieved to see him. The thoughts of murder and dead bodies that I tried so hard to keep at bay had begun creeping up, thanks to Cibil's prediction and Blaire's insistence on talking about it. But one look at Mason and his windblown dark hair, and the thoughts floated away, as insubstantial as vapor.

It was hard to believe I'd once suspected Mason of killing Nathaniel Sharpe. I also couldn't believe I'd ever thought him to be stand-offish, little more than a stereotypical reclusive artist, tortured and lonely. When we'd first met, I'd been trespassing on his property and snooping through his boat house in search of evidence that would point to him being a murderer. So, naturally, I hadn't received the warmest of receptions. Then, we'd met again at Robert Baines' party, and he'd stuck close to my side all night, admitting later that he had wanted to protect me. I felt like a regency romance heroine. Like if Elizabeth Bennett hunted serial killers, but still ended up with Mr. Darcy in the end.

Mason waved to us, his face lighting up in a smile that made my stomach flip. "Did you find anything?"

I narrowed my eyes at him, silently panicking. Did he know I'd been searching the beaches for a sign of another dead body? Was my obsession with murder that obvious?

He pointed to the large, non-descript plastic bag I was carrying. "Looks like you found at least a few things for the B&B."

"Oh, right. Yeah," I said, shaking my head, ridding myself of my paranoia. "I grabbed some bookends and a few vintage books for the bedside tables. No lamps yet, though. I might go online and order some from a few Etsy stores."

Mason nodded and turned to Blaire. "What about you? Did you find anything cool?"

Blaire raised one eyebrow. "In an antique store? No, I didn't."

She slipped into the backseat like a cat, moody and unimpressed. It felt odd considering she'd been so cheerful, even playful, for most of the day. Mason shot me a confused look, and I shrugged, chalking the swift mood change up to teenage hormones.

We melded into the light traffic of cars driving off the ferry, and headed down the main road towards the island's "shopping district." That was what the signage called the area, at least. Though, in reality, it consisted of a General store, a hardware store, a now closed seafood restaurant, a coffee shop called The Drip, and a few gift shops. After a few weeks on the island, I'd found a small grouping of boutiques and antique stores butted up against a residential area towards the back of the island. The shops were all in small, brightly-colored houses that had been renovated into store fronts, making the area feel eclectic, like a hidden gem. I'd been recommending it to the bed and breakfast guests as a replacement for Main Street, hoping to give them a taste of the character the bed and breakfast crowd craved.

I'd been wanting to become more involved with the island's local government—attend city council meetings, petition for more stores and tourist attractions, try to be an active part of improving the island—but the drama of dead bodies and murders had kept me pretty busy. Plus, though no one directly said anything to my face, I had the suspicion that the island somehow blamed me for the sudden upheaval in their quiet society. Though I hadn't directly harmed anyone, I'd been the person who discovered the crimes and, more or less, solved them. Without me, both incidents may have been quietly swept under the rug, which, as bad as it sounds, is what a lot of people prefer to being confronted with the harsh reality that their quiet seaside home has a dark underbelly.

The gravel road that led to the house was as bumpy as ever, my joints feeling as if they could vibrate apart, but as soon as Mason turned into the driveway, it smoothed out. I'd paid an unforgivable amount of money to have the long path to the house paved. Page and I had fought over the issue for a few weeks, but the relief I felt transitioning from the uneven road to the smooth driveway was well worth the cost, and I hoped the guests would think so, as well.

The three story Victorian house faced the road at an angle, the front corner rounding off in a tower that stretched all the way to the attic where Mrs. Harris, the house's previous owner, still lived. That had been another lengthy fight with Page. She hadn't exactly been aware of Mrs. Harris' existence prior to moving in, and when Mrs. Harris welcomed us with delusions and visions of the future, Page was less than thrilled. So far, though, the old woman had been rather quiet. Occasionally, she camped out in front of the window, and I worried her old-world clothing would make the guests believe she was a ghost, but luckily no one had mentioned her slightly unsettling presence yet. The roof was broken into a series of peaks and gables that gave the whole structure nice dimension, and the large porch that wrapped around the front and both sides welcomed guests in like a smile. It had been practically falling apart when we'd first bought the house, sight unseen, but we'd had it repaired to its original state. The intricately carved posts and railings looked like lacework rather than wood, and provided the exact kind of character Page and I had been searching for.

I opened the passenger door and Jasper bounded out of the car and sprinted across the freshly lain grass. We'd gone most of the summer with a dirt yard, but the landscapers had finally laid the sod, and it was amazing how much of an improvement it made. Seeing the place done —save for a few last-minute decorations—made me think, for the first time, that everything could really work out.

"Whose car is that?" Blaire asked, pointing towards the side of the house.

I hadn't noticed the car when we'd pulled up because it was parked under the shade of the large oak tree in the front yard. We had a modest parking lot, but it was already full.

"I'm not sure," I said. "It wasn't here when we left this morning."

I walked closer to the car and noticed the license plate. It was a rental, definitely an out of towner.

"Probably just a last-minute guest," Mason said, brushing it off.

I shook my head. "We are already fully booked. All of the guests are parked in the lot."

Just then, the front door burst open, slamming against the freshly painted siding, and loud voices echoed out across the grass.

"This is outrageous. Absolutely outrageous!" a man shouted, a suitcase swinging wildly in his hand, almost as if he were fixing to shotput it through a window.

Page followed him, her mouth set in a straight line. "I'm sorry, sir. There isn't anything I can do."

"Nothing you can do," the man scoffed, stomping down the front steps. "You could treat your guests with a little respect. That's what you could do!"

"Your check bounced. Perhaps if you had a credit or debit card I could run, I could help. But as it is—" Page's voice trailed off as she saw me, and I noticed her cheeks redden, clearly embarrassed to be caught in such an awkward moment by her daughter and younger sister.

"Even if I did have a credit card, you already gave my

room away! Some service. Take the ferry all the way over here only to find out your room has already been given away. I'll be warning everyone I know away from this place."

The man's bald head was red and sweaty, his neck throbbing with anger. It looked as if he were going to burst any second. Quickly, I jogged across the yard.

"Is there a problem?" I asked, forcing a smile across my face.

The man whipped around and ran his eyes over me, scrutinizing my holey jeans and off the shoulder t-shirt. "It isn't any business of yours," he snapped.

"Actually," I said, clearing my throat. "I'm co-owner of the Sunrise Bed and Breakfast, so I fear it is my business. What seems to be the trouble?"

"Your partner gave my room away without any warning!" he said, pointing an accusatory finger in Page's direction.

Page rose up on her toes, neck outstretched as she tried to explain. "I left several messages, sir—"

"No consideration for my plans at all," the man continued as if Page hadn't spoken. "What am I supposed to do now? The last ferry has already left, and I'm stuck on the island until morning without a place to stay."

Working directly with customers had never been my strong suit. Even as a bank teller, I would run and grab the manager anytime someone had a complaint. But with Page looking at me, frustrated and clearly out of patience, I didn't really have a choice. I was the manager.

"If your payment didn't come through, there really isn't anything we can do. I'm so sorry for the inconvenience, but we can't give away a room for free if there is a paying customer ready and waiting," I said in my most professional voice, trying my best to hide the nervous tremble in my fingers.

The man's mouth opened and closed several times as he processed what I said, trying to work out what to say in response. Then, he released a loud, angry exhale, snorting like a bull before it charges. "Don't make me out to be some free loader! I am more than capable of paying, but my wallet was stolen on the ferry. I'm going to call my bank right now and sort this whole thing out, and when I do, you'll be looking at a lawsuit!"

"That isn't necessary, sir," Mason said, stepping forward. "I'm sure we can work this out."

Just a few months prior I would have given anything for there to be a man in my life willing to step forward and protect me, but at the moment, I just wanted Mason to stay out of it. This was the first complaining customer Page and I were facing, and we had to deal with it ourselves. We had enough doubts in our life without adding customer interaction to the list. Besides, after being attacked by two different murderers and coming out both times with little more than a few scrapes and bruises, I could handle a disgruntled customer.

"There isn't anything to work out," I said, my voice stern, eyes warning Mason to back off. "We are a new business, and as much as we'd love to help you out, sir, there just isn't anything we can do."

The man opened his mouth to speak, but Mason cut him off. "These ladies want to help, but their hands are tied. I, however, have a studio in the back of my house that is open if you need a place to stay. It's small and full of painting supplies, but it's free and it's a roof over your head."

I huffed, annoyed that Mason had continued butting in, despite his offer actually being a good option. It would give the man a place to stay and keep him from taking any legal action against us—even though I didn't truly believe he had a case, the business still didn't need the bad press.

The man, however, didn't seem as impressed. He turned up his lip at Mason, nose in the air. "I'd rather sleep in one of the caves along the coast than take anything from you manipulative people. You come out here and gang up on me. You just watch and wait. People will hear about what a horrible place this is, and you'll be closed down for good."

With that, he grabbed his suitcase and tore off through the yard towards his bright red rental car.

Page shouted apologies after him, but I placed a hand on her shoulder and shook my head. "He isn't worth it, sis. He's a grouch and he isn't going to shut us down. He doesn't have that kind of power."

"You don't know that!" Page said, her voice rising in a panic. "We have no idea who he is or who he knows or what connections he has. I shouldn't have given away his room."

"You were just doing your job," I said, trying to calm her down. "Our job is to keep the rooms full of paying customers and you did that. Job well done."

Page looked at me, unsure, and I could tell she wanted to say something. After a few seconds, however, she turned away, her eyes downcast for a second before she seemed to find her composure.

"You're right. It will all be fine."

"That guy was a jerk, mom," Blaire said, moving forward to loop elbows with her mom and lead her back towards the house.

I watched them walk away.

"Very dramatic evening," Mason said, pulling me into him, wrapping a hand around my waist.

I wanted to lean into him. It had been a few days since we'd seen one another. He'd been commissioned for a huge mural that would act as the centerpiece for a new urban park in Houston, and with the bed and breakfast only being open a few weeks, I barely had time to think about anything else. Still, though, something held me back. Perhaps it was the need to prove to him that I could stand on my own, both figuratively and literally. That I didn't need him defending me or protecting me.

I gently pushed away from him and picked up my shopping bag, which, in the midst of the argument, I'd dropped on the grass. He looked a little spurned, but didn't mention it, and I was relieved. The fight with the guest had drained me, and I didn't want to launch into my 'independent woman' speech just then.

"What are we going to do tonight?" Mason asked, his face expectant, blue eyes wide.

I bit my lower lip. "I was actually thinking I'd hang around here tonight."

He groaned, and grabbed my hand, his thumb tracing a circle around the bone at my wrist. "But we haven't seen each other in ages."

"I know," I said, "but Page has been running the place by herself all day, and with that guy who just left…"

"Will things ever be calm enough for us to hang out again?" he asked, lip jutting out in a pout.

"It's just me and Page. We do everything around here—cooking, cleaning, guest interaction. Life is going to be crazy for a while."

His lips turned up in an almost imperceptible smile, his eyes softening, creasing at the corners. He nodded. "I know. You two work really hard, and I understand that. I just miss you."

My stomach fluttered. I still wasn't entirely certain when Mason and I had decided that we were "a thing." After the crazy night spent in Robert Baines' mansion, eluding death and hunting down a killer, we simply kept in touch. He dropped by the bed and breakfast unannounced to check in, and I'd swing by his studio on my way to run errands to see if he was working on any new paintings and check his progress on the mural. Things had just fallen into a natural rhythm, and now that life was throwing a few obstacles in the way, I wasn't really sure how to get back to that.

"I miss you, too," I said, meaning it. Despite everything I was feeling, I did miss him. But more than anything, I missed what we could have been had our relationship not been, from the outset, surrounded by so much morbidity. I missed the meeting we could have had, where rather than being caught trespassing on his property looking for clues to solve a murder, I could have accidentally backed my cart into his at the general store or driven over to his house to deliver some of his mail that Ed accidentally put in my mailbox.

"I'd tell you to stick around if you wanted, but I'm going to be cleaning bathrooms and serving elderly couples dinner. It's not exactly a glamorous date night," I said.

"Besides," Mason said, "I wouldn't want you to think that counted as quality time. Perhaps a few more days apart will convince you to take a night off and hit the town with me for a real glamorous date night."

"Hit the town?" I asked, imagining the dark, empty stretch of road Sunrise Island considered Main Street. The coffee shop was overrun with teenagers on any weekend, and the next best date place, the General Store, closed at 7 PM on Fridays and Saturdays.

"The city," he said, clarifying, his mouth quirked to the side, amused. "Staying on the island would hardly classify as glamorous."

We talked for another ten to fifteen minutes, the sky over the water rapidly turning pink and then blood orange red before slipping into a pool of inky blacks and blues. Finally, as the lamps inside the bed and breakfast began blinking on one at a time, dousing the lawn in golden light, Mason kissed me on the cheek, reiterated our need for a serious date night, and left.

I made my way across the lawn and up to the porch, hauling the plastic bag of décor I'd bought on the mainland. I could hear a flurry of voices coming from the open sitting room windows. Once it got too dark to be at the beach, the b&b was abuzz with bored, sunburned guests with nowhere else to go. Page had taken to hosting game nights in the sitting room. I was so busy praying they weren't playing Monopoly again and making a mental note to expand our board game collection that I didn't notice the man sitting in the shadow next to the front door.

CHAPTER 4

"Hey there."

I jumped at the sound of the deep voice, nearly dropping my bag through my startled fingers, but just managing to catch it with my hooked index finger before it hit the floor. My lungs had leapt into my throat, and I threw my free hand over my heart, doing my best to regulate its beating.

A man was sitting in one of the low metal deck chairs just to the left of the door. His long legs were relaxed, stretched out in front of him so they nearly reached the edge of the porch. An open book sat in his lap, though I couldn't make out the faded lettering on the spine. He had vivid blonde hair that practically glowed in the darkness, framing his long, square face. Had I not been so terrified, I would have had more energy to appreciate his good looks.

His mouth opened into a small 'o,' matching the wide circles of his eyes.

"I'm sorry," he said, half laughing at my expense. "I didn't mean to startle you."

"What exactly did you mean to do then?" I snapped, my surprise immediately shifting into annoyance. It had to have been clear that I didn't know he was there. Couldn't he have coughed or stamped a foot to alert me to his presence? That was the polite thing to do. Then I had to wonder how long he had been sitting there. Had he seen the argument we'd had with the previous guest? Or had he only come out after Page and Blaire had gone inside, when I was too distracted talking to Mason to notice anyone else come through the front door? Though Mason and I hadn't done anything embarrassing, I felt my cheeks redden at the thought of being watched without knowing it.

The smile faded from his lips, though it didn't fade from his eyes. There was a light behind the caramel brown irises that couldn't be extinguished, even with my clear disapproval.

"I just meant to introduce myself," he said, rising to his feet. "I wanted to meet the person who is so kindly hosting me during my time on the island. You are Piper, are you not?"

I'd noted the length of his legs when he was sitting in the chair, but I was still surprised by his height when he stood up. He towered over me, his head only a foot or so away from brushing against the ceiling. I took a subconscious step back, wondering for a brief second how he knew my name.

Then, I realized he had to be a guest. Though the Bed and Breakfast had been open for a few weeks, I still found myself surprised by the sight of strangers lounging on my sitting room sofa or coming out of the half bath on the first floor. As that realization washed over me, another one followed closely behind. He was a guest, and I'd just been supremely rude to him. That wouldn't be good for the online reviews.

"Oh, gosh," I said, unable to keep my embarrassment to myself. "I'm so sorry. You just surprised me, and my customer service skills aren't great yet. Wow…"

Words seemed to fail me, so I decided to stop speaking, and instead extended my free hand. He offered up a warm smile, his teeth white and straight, and extended an equally warm hand to grasp mine. We stood there for a few seconds longer than was normal, shaking hands and looking at one another. Then, remembering myself (and Mason), I pulled away from him and shoved the traitorous hand in the back pocket of my jeans.

"I didn't catch your name?"

"Jude," he said, running a hand through his wavy blonde hair. "Jude Lawton."

As if his good looks weren't enough, even his name made him sound like the lead character in a romance novel. I tried to ignore all of this, though. Partly because fawning over a man I'd just met strictly based on his good looks made me feel like a teenager, and partly because Mason's soft smile and bright blue eyes kept flashing in my mind like a self-imposed guilt alarm.

When I failed to say anything in return, Jude continued. "Like I said, I didn't intend to startle you. I just wanted to meet you and extend my gratitude for your hospitality."

I smiled at him, hoping it looked more business professional than it felt. "Of course. That is what the Sunrise Bed and Breakfast is here for—to make every guest feel welcome and at home."

"I absolutely feel welcome," he said, nodding his head fervently. "Not too many places would be willing to take in a guy off the street and give him a room without any payment up front. I seriously can't thank you and your sister enough for taking a chance on me. I was afraid I was going to be sleeping in the sand tonight."

Without any payment.

His words floated around in my head like alphabet soup, jumbled, nonsensical. I tried to make sense of it, but kept coming up empty. Hadn't we just kicked a guest out for that exact same reason?

"Right," I said, reluctantly agreeing with him, slowly shaking my head.

I needed to talk to Page.

"Would you excuse me?" I said, lifting up my single bag in explanation. "I need to get this stuff inside."

Jude thanked me again and reclaimed his seat next to the door, picking up what I now realized was a battered copy of *The Adventures of Huckleberry Finn*.

As soon as I walked through the door, Page was on top of me, her hands on my shoulders, spinning me around to face her.

"It's about time. I was afraid I was going to have to go out there and hose you and Mason down to get you to come inside," Page said.

"We were just talking."

"Whatever," she said, waving me away. "It's totally your

turn to entertain the guests. I've been in customer service mode all day and I need a break. Plus, I want to catch up with Blaire. Did everything go okay today? Did she have fun?"

I'd almost forgotten about my scare with losing Blaire just a few hours before, but I knew it was no longer worth mentioning. It would only lead to an unnecessary lecture from Page that I didn't have the energy to deal with. Besides, I had a strong suspicion it was finally my time to lecture Page.

"Everything went fine," I said. "But I actually need to talk to you."

Page was already turning towards the stairs, and she responded over her shoulder. "Can it wait?"

"What's with the guy on the front porch saying he didn't have to pay for his room?" I asked.

Page's shoulders stiffened as she slowly turned back around. The skin under her eyes looked bluer than normal, contrasting with the sudden paleness in her cheeks.

"You met Jude?" she asked, her voice high-pitched in a forced kind of casual.

I nodded. "I met Jude. Who is he? Why isn't he paying?"

"Okay," Page said, taking a step towards me, her voice lowering. "I know what you're thinking."

"That we just kicked a man out for not paying and now we have another one?"

"Yes," Page said, nodding. "That. I know that's what you're thinking, but Jude is different."

"If by different, you mean Jude looks like the clean

shaven single dad in a romcom while the other guy looks like a used cars salesman, then yes, they are different. In every other way, though, they are the exact same. We don't make any money by either of them staying here." I was still talking quietly, but my whisper had grown harsher and harsher as I spoke until I sounded like the hiss from a hot kettle.

"You aren't listening," Page said, using her mom voice on me, trying to make me feel like I was overreacting. "You're jumping to conclusions."

"And you're giving away rooms for free," I snapped. "You're meant to be the responsible one between us, remember?"

I rarely ever pointed out this dynamic between us, but it was mostly because it didn't need to be pointed out. Anyone who spent any amount of time with the Lane sisters knew that I was the free-spirit, the screw up, and Page held everything together. What was going to happen to the Sunrise Bed and Breakfast if Page forgot that?

"I'm not giving it away," Page said, finally raising her voice, apparently not used to being the one on trial. "He's going to pay us tomorrow.

I paused, waiting for her to continue explaining, but she didn't elaborate. Page crossed her arms over her chest protectively and alternated looking at me and the floor.

"And why didn't he pay today?" I asked.

Page hesitated. "He didn't have the money today."

Once again, I waited for her to elaborate, and once again, she stayed silent. I sighed. "You're going to need to explain this situation to me more fully if you want me to understand, Page. Why didn't he have the money today?"

Her posture unfurled like a scroll, and the words spilled out of her.

"He showed up unannounced just after you and Blaire left this morning. He was looking for a place to stay while he did some work on the island. If he'd shown up even an hour earlier I would have had to send him away because we were full, but I'd just discovered that Mr. Bergeron's payment had failed to go through, so, based on policy, his room was available."

Page paused, as though waiting for my confirmation that she had done nothing wrong in giving Mr. Bergeron's room to Jude. I, however, remained stoic, aware that I was enjoying Page's vulnerable position a bit more than I probably should be. Seeing that she still had a long way to go before I was convinced, Page quickly resumed her story.

"I told him we only had one room left, but it was one of the bigger rooms with a private bathroom, so it would cost a little more than our standard rate. He said that was fine, as long as it was okay that he couldn't pay up front. I told him I didn't know if I could do that, but he explained that he had come to the island for a business opportunity and he would have money the next day—cash. Of course, I felt a little nervous about it, but he was going to be staying in our most expensive room, and I didn't want to lose out on the money. Mr. Bergeron had the place reserved for a week, and I didn't want it to sit empty, so I told him a late payment would be fine and I checked him in."

"You mean you checked him out," I said, raising an eyebrow at her.

She flushed, her lips set in a stern line. "That's not fair, Piper. You didn't even listen to my reasons for—"

"No, I heard you," I said. "I just don't believe you. I'd be less annoyed if you were being honest with me. It's really not as complicated as you're making it out to be. You let him stay here because he's a total babe."

"You're a child," Page said, twisting her mouth to one side and glancing towards the sitting room where the guests were playing a rousing board game. Mrs. Smith, a woman in her mid-70s, had just landed on a space that announced the birth of her twin girls, and she was gingerly placing the tiny plastic children in the back of her lime green minivan.

Then, Page's focus shifted back to me for a second before her face fell completely blank. It looked as though someone had hit the factory reset button on her brain, and she was in the middle of rebooting. Her eyes went glassy, mouth hanging open slightly, and she swayed on the spot as though her muscles had lost the ability to hold her up. Then, all at once, she snapped back into sharp focus, looking normal, if a little flushed.

I looked around, wondering what had bothered her so much, and found my answer standing in the doorway.

"Hi, Jude," I said biting back a laugh despite my embarrassment.

He was standing up straight, but somewhere in the back of my mind he was leaning against the door frame, shirt unbuttoned and flapping in a sudden gust of wind. And based on Page's dopey expression when I turned around, the same image had been playing in her head.

He smiled at us, and then ducked his head and tip toed

towards the stairs, gesturing towards the other guests in the sitting room. "I'd stay and chat, but Mrs. Smith has been trying to get me to play strip poker with her all day."

Page released a quick howl of laughter and then choked it back, wiping a hand across her mouth. Jude winked at her and went up the stairs to his room.

"How does he look?" I asked, elbowing Page in the side.

She shook her head as if she were waking up from a deep sleep. "What?"

"Well there is no way you're not picturing him in nothing but his boxers right now, so I just wanted to know how good he looks," I said, loving how flustered Jude made Page.

Page turned to me, her face serious and harsh, the crease between her eyebrows deepening. "Could you stop acting like a teenager?"

"You said I was acting like a child a minute ago, so this is a step up. Give me an hour and maybe I'll finally be acting like an adult," I snickered.

Sensing the productive portion of our conversation had ended, Page rolled her eyes at me and stomped up the stairs to her room.

"Mrs. Smith," I said, stepping into the sitting room, "those are some beautiful baby girls you've got there."

Mrs. Smith picked up her tiny plastic car and pressed it to her cheek. "Who would've thought an old gal like me would be a mother again?" she said.

By the end of the game, she had two more children, a boy and a girl, and she'd retired a millionaire.

CHAPTER 5

The guests were slow to wake the next morning, and I was grateful, rushing around the kitchen flipping pancakes, slicing grapefruit, and pouring mug after mug of coffee. Page regularly helped with breakfast, though we both knew I was the better cook, but this morning when I'd knocked on her door, she'd cracked it open, her wet hair twisted into a towel, and asked if I could handle it alone. As much as I didn't want to, I felt only slightly bad about teasing her over Jude the night before, so I'd agreed. Now, though, as the guests were filtering downstairs and I could hear their voices growing steadily louder from the dining room, I regretted it.

Blaire walked in, low rise jeans barely slung across her hips, her shirt riding up to just under her belly button.

"Good morning, Christina Aguilera," I said, eying her warily.

Blaire rolled her eyes and took the coffee pot from my hand and filled her travel mug.

"Are you leaving already?" I asked, glancing at the clock and seeing that it was just a few minutes past eight.

She nodded and slurped her black coffee before it could pour over the rim, wincing at the bitter flavor. "Matthew is working at the Marina today and I'm going to go with him."

Matthew was Blaire's boyfriend of the past few months. They'd met our first week on the island and had been inseparable ever since. Matthew's parents, Greg and Tillie Pelkey, owned the island's marina. I'd had the distinct pleasure of meeting them for the first time at Robert Baines' party. As dead bodies were discovered, and everyone realized there was a murderer amongst us, Greg drank most of the bar cart by himself and Tillie chain smoked until the police finally arrived early the next morning. They both clearly had their vices and I only hoped Matthew didn't have his own. He seemed nice enough, but if he was dating Blaire, nice enough simply wasn't enough. He needed to be perfect.

"It looks like a brunch bomb went off in here. Do you need any help?" she asked.

I was thinking how sweet it was of her to offer her help, but before I could respond, Blaire grabbed the lid to her travel mug, and said, "Great. Good luck. See you for dinner!"

"How considerate!" I shouted after her, hoping she felt at least a little guilty for leaving me to handle breakfast by myself.

Fifteen minutes later, just as I'd finished my fifth trip to the dining room, arms loaded down with the last of the cream, sugar, and butter for the table, I heard a clicking on the tile and turned to see Page enter the kitchen.

"Whoa," I said, leaning back, eyes wide, looking Page up and down.

"What?" she said, shrugging me off a little too casually.

She'd traded in her usual slacks and flowy button down for a forest green wrap dress that hugged the small of her waist and brought out flecks of yellow in her eyes. Then, as if that wasn't bizarre enough, her sensible black flats had been upgraded to high heels.

"I thought high heels were torture devices invented by creepy men to make it harder for women to run away," I said, repeating something Page had said to me too many times to count.

"Do you see any creepy men around?" she said, challenging me. When I continued smirking at her, she rolled her eyes. "Shut up, Piper."

"I didn't say anything," I said, hands raised in the air in surrender. Honestly, it was nice to see Page excited about a guy. She'd expressed a desire, once or twice, to start dating, but I wasn't sure if she ever would. She hadn't been on a date in almost twenty years, and that had been with the man she divorced after sixteen years of marriage. So, she was understandably hesitant to trust another man.

She walked into the dining room and I followed behind her like a spectator at a golf tournament, keeping my distance, silently standing on the sidelines, and eager to see what would happen.

Jude was sitting at the head of the long dining room table, two slices of plain buttered toast and a grapefruit in front of him. Page approached him, her hips moving more than I'd ever seen them move before, and gestured to the chair next to him, a question in her eyes.

Jude smiled, looking her up and down once, and nodded. She lowered herself into the chair. "Just toast?"

"I can't handle too much sugar so early in the morning," he said. "It makes me feel sluggish."

I gave Jude one mental tally in the pro column. Page was a health nut, and, after spending so many years married to a man who thought the filling in a Pop-Tart counted towards his daily fruit intake, being someone whose diet more closely resembled hers would be a nice change of pace.

"I'm the same way," she said. "But I can't get Piper to stop making pancakes and waffles."

I hadn't expected to be mentioned in their conversation, so when Page and Jude turned to look at me, I felt like a child being caught listening at the door. I smiled awkwardly back at them, unsure whether I should admit that I had been eavesdropping or pretend I hadn't heard.

"You have a sweet tooth, then?" Jude asked, ending my internal debate and officially welcoming me into their conversation.

"A bit," I said, smiling and trying to maintain my distance. I wanted Page to talk to Jude on her own without my interference.

"A bit?" Page asked, her eyes rolling in my direction. "You used to put chocolate milk in your cereal."

I suddenly remembered what Blaire had told me about Page eating three King-sized candy bars, and had Jude not been sitting right there, I would have mentioned it, thereby earning the right to eat whatever junk I wanted in front of her in peace. Instead, I shrugged and smiled, making a mental note to inform Page later of how much exactly she owed me for being the world's best wing woman.

"I like chocolate." I tried to give her a piercing stare as I spoke, hoping that somehow the telepathy we'd tried so hard to use as kids would finally kick in and she'd realize that I knew her dirty little candy bar secret. But Page remained blissfully ignorant of my knowledge, and I let it go, trying to sink back into the freshly painted navy-blue walls.

"There's no shame in that," Jude said. "My sister drank chocolate milk by the gallon throughout her entire pregnancy."

"Oh, you're an uncle?" Page asked.

"Several times over."

Page hesitated and I could anticipate her next question before she even said it. I'd noticed her eyes darting to his ring finger, as if a ring might appear there between glances. "Do you have any kids of your own?"

Jude's mouth quirked up on the side, but he bit it back and shook his head. "No. No children of my own. Maybe one day."

Page nodded, a thousand more questions burning in her eyes. But before she could say anything, Jude continued.

"If I ever find the right woman that is."

Page lit up, and I noticed her shoulders relax.

"You have a daughter, though, right?" Jude asked, his

eyes going stormy as the words came out. "Or did I read your relationship entirely wrong and make an idiot of myself?"

Page laughed. "Blaire is my daughter."

"Thank heaven," Jude said.

Page reached out and touched his shoulder, still laughing, and my heart lurched. I felt so creepy watching them, but it was like a romance movie playing out before my eyes. Just as it was getting good, though, I noticed someone shuffle into the room.

Mrs. Harris was wrapped in her ratty gray shawl, and her eyes were unseeing orbs. Mrs. Smith instinctively reached out to grab Mr. Smith's arm, and they slid their chairs closer together. The bright, cheerful vibe seemed to have been sucked from the room, and suddenly everyone's eyes were glued to their plates.

Miraculously, despite Page's strong aversion to Mrs. Harris living in the attic, she was so wrapped up in Jude that she didn't notice, and I wanted to keep it that way. Quickly, I walked around the table and wrapped an arm around Mrs. Harris' shoulder.

"Good morning," I said, smiling at her, though she didn't seem to register I had even spoken to her.

"I have your breakfast in the kitchen," I said, leading her gently towards the kitchen door.

"Darkness," Mrs. Harris said, her voice harsh and raspy.

Abigail, the middle-aged woman who had checked into the bed and breakfast to work on the first draft of her romance novel, was watching Mrs. Harris out of the corner of her eye, trying her hardest not to openly stare at the old woman.

"Okay," I said, my voice cheery and light.

"Darkness lurks here," Mrs. Harris said, moving her hands in the air as though she were gesturing to a crystal ball.

"I just haven't opened all the blinds yet," I said, prodding Mrs. Harris slightly less gently towards the kitchen door. "That must be what you see."

"Anger. Violence," she continued, completely ignoring me.

Once we made it into the kitchen I kicked the stopper out from under the door and let it swing closed behind us. Mrs. Harris had caused remarkably few issues with the guests, but her presence always unnerved people. Page made me explain Mrs. Harris' living situation to every guest before handing them the keys so they wouldn't be alarmed if they encountered her in the hallway.

"They'll think she's the ghost of an ancient witch," Page said. "We can't let innocent people wander around this house without knowing what to expect."

"She's an old woman, not a demon," I said, though Page's dubious look said that she wasn't entirely certain.

I helped Mrs. Harris into a stool at the kitchen island and dropped a plate of pancakes in front of her. Immediately, all talk of evil and darkness stopped, and she tucked into the food, dripping syrup on the granite. I wanted to go back into the dining room and listen to Page and Jude talk while pretending to fawn over pictures of Mr. and Mrs. Smith's eight grandchildren, but leaving Mrs. Harris alone was a bad idea, particularly so early in the morning. She seemed more energetic in the mornings.

By the time Mrs. Harris was inching up the stairs to the attic and I made it back to the dining room, the guests had finished eating and Page was beginning to pick up plates to carry into the kitchen. Jude was gone.

"Well?" I prodded, raising my eyebrows at her.

"Well what?" Page asked, her mouth twisted into a tight knot, a smile burning in her eyes.

"Oh, don't be a tease, Page. You know what."

A smile broke across her face. "He wants me to show him around the island tonight."

I raised one fist in the air in a gesture of victory. "That's amazing. Why tonight?"

"He didn't come to the island just to date me," Page said, suddenly defensive. "He has work to do. He was busy. It doesn't mean anything that he put it off. First dates are typically in the evening anyway, so—"

"Whoa, whoa," I said, touching her shoulder. "Easy. I wasn't suggesting anything. What I meant was: 'What does he have going on today?'"

Page took a deep yogic inhale and exhale, and seemed much steadier for it. "All he said is that he had some business to attend to and that he'd be back this evening before dinner."

"*Business to attend to,*" I said, my nose lifted in the air. "He sounds so important and businessy."

"And cute, too," Page whispered, eyes darting around in case another guest was nearby.

"Very," I said, nodding enthusiastically.

"Don't get any ideas," she said, winking at me. "You have your own man."

"I suppose so, though me and my man haven't spent any time together in almost a week."

Page's face turned suddenly serious, her eyebrows drawing together. She leaned an elbow on the counter top and turned her body to face mine. "Are you two doing okay? I didn't realize anything was wrong."

I forced a laugh. "Okay. First of all, this is not a therapy session. Second, nothing is wrong. I just said we haven't hung out lately. That doesn't mean anything is wrong."

Page shook her head. "It's not a sign that things are right."

Now I was the defensive one. "We've both been busy with work. Couples can be busy and still love one another."

Her entire face lit up the way it used to when she found my hiding spot during hide and seek. "You love each other?"

"Hold on," I said, raising a hand to stop her thought in its tracks, but it was useless. Page was taking my slip up and running with it.

"You said you love him!" She smooched her lips together, smacking them loudly.

Despite my annoyance, I couldn't help but laugh. Page was rarely ever giddy or silly, especially since we'd moved to the island, and though her laughter was at my expense, I didn't want to be the one to silence it.

"Now you are the one acting like a child," I said, shaking my head and scrubbing a syrup-covered plate.

"And you are the one in love," she said as she snagged a blueberry muffin from the table and headed for the door.

"Those are full of sugar," I shouted after her. "And I used white flour instead of whole wheat."

She spun in a circle and took a huge bite out of the muffin, nearly eating the entire top. "My sister is in love! I'm celebrating!"

CHAPTER 6

After several weeks of cooking for the guests, I still hadn't figured out exactly how much food to order for a house full of people. So, my weekly last-minute trips to the General Store had become almost routine. We ordered all of our supplies and ingredients in bulk from a store on the mainland, and had everything shipped over on the ferry, but that morning's pancakes had wiped out our stores of syrup and butter.

It was mid-morning on a weekday, so the beaches were full of vacationers and the elderly and retired, but Main Street was a ghost town. The coffee shop down the road had a few people milling around in front of it, sipping on steaming hot cups of coffee, despite the temperature being well over ninety degrees even before noon, but otherwise, my car was the only one parked on the street.

Katie was running the cash register today. She had

three kids at home and her engineer husband made more than enough money for her to stop working, but getting out of the house a few days every week kept her sane. Or, at least, that's what she'd told me one of the first times I came into the store and asked her how her day was going. Now I knew better than to engage Katie in a conversation if I had anywhere to be within the next hour. With three kids at home under the age of five, I couldn't blame her for craving a bit of adult conversation, but still, I had things to do.

"Hey, Pipes," she said, calling me by the nickname she'd christened me with (without my consent) the first time we'd met. "Those guests eating you out of house and home again?"

"They each ate way more than their fair share of syrup," I said.

"We have regular and lite syrup on the shelves near the oatmeal, but we also have maple syrup in the glass jars in the organic section," she said. "Though, I'd imagine those are a bit expensive to serve to the bed and breakfasters. My husband doesn't think anyone should spend ten dollars on syrup, but it tastes so much better. Have you ever been to Vermont? We went there for vacation— before the kids, of course—and stayed at a little inn that served the fluffiest buttermilk waffles you've ever seen and had the fanciest syrups. Blueberry and raspberry syrup! Have you ever heard of such a thing? But their maple syrup was to die for. I bought a bottle from the chef before we left. It cost me fifteen dollars, but it was amazing. I still have the glass bottle. It was shaped like a Maple leaf. Mabel puts her marbles in it. HA! That sounds like a tongue twister."

Her words washed over me like a tidal wave—too large to swim, so I let the current take me away—and I smiled and nodded as I raided the store's supply of syrup. I opted for five bottles of regular and three of lite.

I gathered the bottles precariously in my arms and waddled to the front of the store where I unloaded them on the table between a rack of lighters with seascapes painted on the sides and several boxes of fifty cent gum.

"Is this everything?" she asked, already scanning the syrup.

I almost nodded yes when I remembered the butter. "Oh, shoot. No," I said, turning and jogging towards the refrigerated section. "I forgot the butter."

"We have sticks of butter next to the cream cheese or the vegetable oil knock off stuff next to the shredded cheese. Personally? I like the sticks of butter. I know they say it's bad for your health and such, but it can't be worse for me than the thousand and one ingredients they use to make that Frankenstein butter. You know? Of course, no offense if that's the kind of butter you like to use. Everyone has their own preference."

I grabbed a tub of the "Frankenstein butter," as Katie had so succinctly called it, and walked back to the register.

"Now are you sure this is everything?" she asked again, a laugh in her voice.

I nodded. "Positive."

By some kind of miracle, Katie rang up the rest of my

items, bagged them, and accepted my card without any conversation. I was beginning to think I would make it out of the store without being pulled into one of her tirades. However, just as I looped the plastic bag handles over my wrists and lifted them off the register, she spoke.

"You know, I actually had a guy come in here yesterday just before closing. His card was declined and he wanted me to give him a pack of cigarettes for free. He tried buttering me up, but I'm married, you know, and I don't go around flirting with strange men. So obviously, I told him I couldn't do that. Then he asked to use the phone. It's supposed to be only for employees and never for personal calls, but I was afraid to tell him no again, so I let him. Whoever he called didn't pick up, but he left a message. He was talking really quietly, and I tried to listen in, but I could only catch bits and pieces. It had something to do with a bank account—probably in relation to his card being declined—and getting a boat in the morning." She stopped and rolled her eyes. "When he hung up the phone, I told him the ferry was free and he didn't need any money to ride it, but you know what he did? He gave me a real nasty look and told me to mind my own business. Not a nice man. Not a nice man at all."

"Did you catch who he was?" I asked, wondering whether it wasn't the same guy we'd kicked out of the bed and breakfast the day before.

"I think he had brown hair, but it was hard to tell because he had a baseball cap on. I should have known he would be rude when he first walked in. No gentleman wears a ball cap inside. My husband is coaching my youngest son's tee ball team, and one of the first things he taught them was to remove their hat indoors and when the National Anthem plays. Of course, they don't play the National Anthem at Tee Ball games, but still, it's a good lesson to learn."

It was clear I'd lost Katie to another tangent, and I wasn't going to get much more information out of her, so I quickly grabbed my bags and began moving towards the door, smiling and nodding as she spoke. As soon as she paused for a breath, I wished her a good day and ducked out onto the sidewalk.

As soon as the door shut behind me, I turned and crashed into a large, solid man, and stumbled backwards, catching myself on the doorframe.

"So sorry," I said, righting myself.

"I think I can manage to forgive you," a low, smooth voice said.

I looked up into Jude's square face.

"Oh, hi," I said, relieved it was someone I knew. "I guess I ought to look out where I'm going."

He shrugged. "Trust me, there are worse things than running into a Lane girl on the street."

I blushed and felt ashamed of myself. Not only was Jude the first guy my sister had shown any interest in since her divorce, but Mason was the guy who was supposed to make me blush.

"What brings you to our island's most popular one stop shop?" I asked, gesturing to the general store window, which also advertised for a hardware store located at the back of the building.

He smiled, and his perfectly white teeth actually glinted in the sunshine. "Just picking up a few things."

"You are so mysterious," I said, narrowing my eyes at him.

"Am I?"

I nodded and pursed my lips. "Page said you left because you had 'business to attend to,' and now you are just 'picking up a few things.' It's tough to get a straight answer out of you."

"You two were talking about me?" he asked, a mischievous smile spreading across his face.

Oh no. Was that the wrong thing to say? Had I made Page look desperate by admitting that we'd talked about him? She would kill me if she knew I was talking to him about her. Worse yet, she'd kill me if she knew I was talking to him at all while, at the same time, being incapable of ignoring how incredibly handsome he was.

"There you go again," I joked. "Changing the subject."

He was about to respond with what I'm sure would have been a witty response, but the General Store door opened and Katie stuck her long, thin neck through the opening.

"They found a body," she said, breathless.

The words stuck in my throat, though I hadn't been the one to speak them. Suddenly, it felt as if I'd tried to swallow an entire sleeve of salty crackers without a drop of water.

"A body?" Jude repeated, asking the question I was too

afraid to, his brown eyes going dark, indistinguishable from his pupils.

Katie nodded. "I just heard it on the police scanner in the store. Boss says the scanner is a distraction and pointless because the island is small enough that everyone knows what's going on within a few minutes of it happening anyway, but I like to keep it nearby just in case something ever happens at my house or at the daycare where my kids go—"

"Katie!" I shouted, finding my voice, unable to take another second of Katie's ramblings about anything and everything but the topic at hand. "What were you saying about a body?"

She looked startled by my outburst, but finally began relaying what little information she'd gathered from the scanner.

"A jet skier found a body in one of the caves along the shoreline on the east side of the island. He rode back to the Marina and called it in to the police."

Jude's face had gone white while Katie was talking and it looked as though he might pass out. I reached out a hand to touch his shoulder, steady him.

"What's going on?"

I whipped around, startled by the sudden voice, to find Mason turning the corner, a giant roll of canvas under his arm and a box of paints in the other.

His eyes were darting suspiciously between me and Jude, and I instinctively dropped my hand from his shoulder.

"A body was found on the beach," Katie said eagerly. She might as well have been an old-time newspaper boy shouting about breaking news on the street corner. *EXTRA! EXTRA! READ ALL ABOUT IT!*

"Who is it?" Mason asked, moving closer to me, wedging himself between me and Jude. "Are you alright, Piper?"

"I'm fine. It doesn't have anything to do with me," I said, grateful that there was finally a body with no connection to me or my family or my business.

Just as that thought crossed my mind, though, I remembered what Katie had said.

"You said the police were going to the Marina?"

Katie nodded. "They're going to make it their head-quarters since it's so close to where the body was found."

I sighed. "Blaire is at the Marina with Matthew. I should go check on her and see if she needs a ride home."

Jude had barely said two words since Katie had delivered the news about the body, and he looked stricken, like he'd eaten some bad shrimp and was moments away from spewing everywhere.

"Are you okay?" I asked him. "Do you need a ride anywhere?"

"I can take you anywhere you need to go, man," Mason said, jumping in to help. Though his offer was kind, I had a feeling it had a lot more to do with me than it did with wanting to help Jude. Especially since, up until a few seconds before, he'd never seen Jude in his life.

Jude shook his head. "No, I'm fine. Just surprised is all."

"At the rate bodies keep popping up around here, it would be more surprising if they hadn't found a body," Katie said with a laugh.

Upon seeing my face, though, she sobered. "Sorry."

It seemed Katie did have at least a modicum of self-control.

"I need to get going," Jude said, glancing down at his watch and then taking off down the street without waiting for anyone to respond.

"He seemed kind of weird," Mason said, whispering in my ear.

"He's a very nice guy," I said. "He was just in shock."

Mason nodded, but I could see the hurt flare up behind his eyes. I knew he was being ridiculous—Jude was interested in Page, and I would never do anything to hurt my sister—but he didn't know that. We hadn't exactly set the parameters of our relationship, anyway. For all Mason knew, we weren't exclusive and I'd been dating around behind his back.

"Most people aren't accustomed to finding dead bodies at the rate we are," I said, nudging him with my elbow, trying to make light of what was a very heavy situation.

Mason gave me a half-hearted smile. "Do you want me to go to the Marina with you?"

"No, it's okay. You seem pretty busy," I said, gesturing to the painting supplies in his arms, "and I'm just going to swing by and check on Blaire before heading back to the B&B."

"I don't mind," he said. "I just had to make a run for more supplies. I have some time."

"Really, Mason," I said, running my hand down his forearm, trying to convey to him how okay we were. "It will take a few minutes and I'll be home again. It wouldn't be worth your time."

He shrugged. "If you're sure."

"I am," I said.

We looked at each other for a second, unspoken words flowing between us. Then, someone cleared their throat.

At the same time, Mason and I turned to find Katie still standing in the doorway of the General Store, staring at us blankly as though she were watching a television show. I raised my eyebrows at her, and it took her a few seconds, but she seemed to awaken, as if from a dream, and look away.

"Oh, um, sorry," she said, pivoting away from us. "I'll leave you two be. I hope Blaire is alright, Piper. And Mason…well, bye."

After she left and the door slammed closed behind her, the bell hanging inside the door tinkling softly, Mason finally smiled a real smile. "That was the first time I've ever seen Katie not know what to say."

"Apparently all it takes is a really awkward moment and a good dose of shame," I joked.

Mason kissed me once, quickly, and then walked down the street to his car. I watched him go until I began to feel like an overly dramatic character in a romance movie, and got into my own car, throwing the syrup and butter in the backseat.

Despite knowing I was going down to the Marina just to check on Blaire and leave again, something about being so close to the active investigation of yet another body on Sunrise Island made me uncomfortable. I didn't want to be involved, and I certainly didn't want to see another corpse. My body felt tense, ready for anything, but I was trying desperately to convince my nervous system that it didn't need to worry. The Marina was just going to be a stop on my way home. I was going to spend the afternoon making beds, cleaning bathrooms, and prepping breakfast for the next morning. Nothing weird or murderous would happen at all. I was certain of it.

CHAPTER 7

The Marina was usually rather busy. Anyone who lived on the island typically did so, in part, because of the direct access to water they had, so the residents and visitors to Sunrise Island frequented the Marina to check out jet skis and tubes or to dock their own boats. Today, though, the place was flooded with people.

Cars were parked in the lot, but also all down the road leading to the Marina, and many people were on foot. People in dark blue uniforms and matching hats, clearly having something to do with the investigation, were carrying large plastic cases towards the shore. Small clusters of men in fishing hats and carrying tackle boxes stood against the Marina wall, checking their watches and shaking their heads.

I stopped my car in the driveway and got out.

"You can't park there," one of the fishermen said, exasperated.

"I'm just running inside for a second," I said.

"No, you're not. They aren't letting anyone take any boats in or out," he said.

I smiled at him as I passed by. "I'm not here for a boat."

He called after me as I walked through the Marina's main office door. "You still can't park there."

The sheriff, Shep, was leaning against the wall, looking tired. He tipped his hat towards me as I walked in. Blaire was sitting behind the main receptionist desk, Matthew right beside her, the phone pressed to his ear.

"I don't know what's going on," he said. "But I need you or dad to come down here right now."

As I walked in, he gave me a weary smile that quickly fell to an annoyed grimace. "I don't think the police care that you have a hair appointment," he said.

Blaire stood up and walked around the desk to me.

"What are you doing here?" she asked, talking in a whisper, though I didn't know why.

"It's lovely to see you, too, dear niece," I joked.

She tilted her head to the side, clearly already annoyed with my presence.

"I heard they found a body, so I came down to make sure you were okay."

"Did you think I was dead or something? Because you don't seem nearly relieved enough to see me alive and well, if that were the case. Also, since when do you have a police scanner?"

I explained everything to her, Katie, the General Store, Jude and Mason.

"Wow," she said when I was done. "It's a miracle you made it here so quickly. Katie never shuts up."

"That's not nice," I said, reprimanding her, though I

couldn't tell her it wasn't true. I was still surprised I'd made it in and out of the store within twenty minutes. "What's going on here?"

She sighed. "We don't know. There's a body, but they aren't telling us anything else because they want to speak to an adult. Matthew is eighteen, but that doesn't seem to mean much to them because he's still in high school. Though," she said, raising her voice and angling her head towards Shep, "*LEGALLY* he is an adult."

I smiled an apology at Shep and he gave me a knowing look that said something along the lines of, *"teenagers, am I right?"*

"Then call dad!" Matthew shouted into the phone. "This is your business, and the police are here asking for you. They won't talk to me. Figure it out amongst yourselves."

He slammed the phone down into the receiver and then looked up at Shep, a false smile dripping from his lips. "They will be here shortly."

Shep nodded and turned towards me. "I'd actually like to talk to you when you have a minute. I'll wait outside."

He left and Blaire followed him with her eyes, mouth hanging open.

"How is it that everyone is always willing to talk to you, but they won't give us the time of day? Matthew works here and I spend most of my time here, but somehow, we are further down on the totem pole than you are? How is that fair?"

"You don't even know what he wants to say to me. It could be about anything," I said.

"Not likely. You always have your hand in the murder investigations around here. So not fair."

I wanted to remind Blaire that my life had been threatened on more than one occasion, that I'd had to kill a man to save my own skin, and that I'd never asked for any of this. I wanted to tell her how tired I was of the non-stop excitement and chaos. I just wanted to run my business and hang out with my boyfriend, or whatever Mason was to me, and not constantly worry about someone dying. But I didn't say any of that because, regardless of what Blaire thought, she wasn't an adult yet. She deserved to be protected, at least for a little while longer.

"Life's not fair, kid," I said, reminding myself of my dad. "Do you want a ride home? It looks like things might be a little crazy around here."

"No, I'm helping Matthew."

I glanced at Matthew for confirmation, looking to see whether Blaire's presence was more helpful or stressful, but he just stared at me blankly.

"Okay," I said finally. "Call if you change your mind."

"I won't," she said.

I turned to leave, but just before I opened the door, Blaire called after me. She rolled her eyes, but her mouth was turned up in a small smile. "Thanks for checking on me, Aunt Piper."

"Of course," I said.

Shep was waiting just outside the door, and he began talking almost as soon as I stepped out of the office.

"Okay, so a jet skier found a body in a nearby cave. He had a pretty mean dent on the right side of his head, which is likely what did him in. No wallet or ID on him."

The words hung between us, heavy and expectant.

Finally, after several seconds of silence, I shrugged. "Okay?"

He widened his eyes at me. "Well, what do you think?"

"Umm…I think that's a real shame. Someone ought to crack down on the crime around here."

He sighed. "I mean, what do you think happened? Any clues or anything?"

I couldn't believe what I was hearing. Was the sheriff coming to me to help him solve this murder investigation? Surely, I was misunderstanding something.

"Are you asking me to help you solve this case?"

Suddenly Shep seemed uncertain, he crossed and uncrossed his arms, his feet shifting. "Well, no. But, I mean, if you have any insights, it would be nice of you to share them with me."

"I'm not a detective, Shep. Or a police officer or a medical examiner or anyone with any sort of authority here. I can't help you."

"Sure you can," he said. "You're like…what's that guy's name from that one show? He's an author who helps solve murder cases and then writes books about them? You're like one of those people. A regular person who helps the police solve cases."

"No, Shep, I'm really not. I'm a regular person. Period."

Shep looked confused. "I thought this was kind of your thing."

"Not by choice. I didn't choose to get wrapped up in

murder cases. It just happened. But this one is on you," I said. "You don't need my help, anyway."

Bolstered by my praise, Shep lifted his head and nodded. "Yeah, I know. I just thought maybe you'd want to help, but I can do it on my own."

"I know you can, Shep. You'll have this one solved in no time."

I didn't actually believe this. Maggie Summerfield's murder had been classified as an accidental drowning for years before I figured out it was Martin Little. There was no saying that Shep wouldn't come to the same conclusion with this case. However, that wasn't my business.

Shep strode off in the direction of a police boat—something I never thought existed before moving to Sunrise Island—his tan pants sporting a bright blue stain on the back of his left leg, presumably from an exploded pen. Normally I would have chased after him and told him about the spot, but at the moment, I simply didn't have the energy. I'd left the house for syrup and butter and had somehow ended up making my complicated relationship with Mason ever so slightly more complicated, driven halfway across the island to make sure my niece was okay being so close to a murder investigation, and turned down a volunteer detective position from the island's sheriff—which didn't exactly leave me overflowing with confidence in my local police force. The day had gone too many places I didn't expect, and I just wanted to be back home.

I walked back to my car, passing by the old fisherman who had complained about my parking job and tossing him an insincere smile. As I was about to open the driver's side door and climb in, I noticed the car next to me for the first time. It was Matthew's.

Immediately my mind flashed to a conversation I'd had with Page. We'd been discussing whether or not Blaire should have her own car on the island. She depended pretty heavily on Matthew driving her around, and despite buying her a bike the first week we moved to the island, Blaire refused to use it. I knew it had something to do with being a teenager and maintaining her image, but I didn't understand how riding a bike could be embarrassing unless, of course, you fell off the bike in front of all of your friends. I had been leaning pretty heavily towards getting her a car. She would need a car when she left for college anyway, and her dad had expressed an interest in paying for her first car.

"He's trying to buy her love, Piper. I'm not going to let him do that," Page had said.

"Why not? You know Blaire can't be bought, and this way, you will have been the one who allowed him to pay for it. You get all of the cool parent points without forking over any of the money. Win win."

"I read an article that said teenagers are most likely to hide things from their parents in their cars. It makes sense. It's the only place outside of the home that the parent doesn't really have access to. I don't want to buy her a hiding spot," Page said.

"First of all," I responded, "you won't be buying it. Second, how was this study conducted? Did they ask a bunch of teenagers? Because, if so, I can almost guarantee the teenagers lie. Why would they give up their best kept secret? Third, do you not trust Blaire?"

Page hadn't answered me, but apparently she didn't trust Blaire because she still didn't have a car and we never talked about it again.

Now, I was still rather dubious about whichever article it was that Page had read that claimed to know teenagers' deepest secrets, but that still didn't keep me from wondering what Matthew had hidden in his own car. From what I knew of his parents, they weren't exactly the PTO types, and he seemed to have a lot of freedoms. And while I wanted to trust Blaire and believe he was a stand-up guy, there was really no telling until I did a little digging myself. It was my job as her aunt after all, right?

As nonchalantly as possible, I slipped around the back of my car and opened the rear passenger door, pretending to be looking for something in the backseat. After a few careful glances around the area to be sure no one was watching me too closely, I spun around and peered through the grimy, dirt-streaked window of Matthew's car.

The first thing I noticed was the filth. There was no other word to describe it. The layer of grease and dirt over everything wasn't merely untidy or dirty, it was filthy. Unidentifiable stains covered nearly every surface of the interior, and open food containers were strewn around the backseat in various stages of decay.

Amongst the trash and food containers, I spotted a wallet. This wouldn't have been unusual except I spotted several of them. Five, in total. And then, underneath an opened sour cream and cheddar chip bag, was a black fanny pack. Based on what I knew about Matthew and fashion for the last two decades, fanny packs weren't a staple wardrobe item for most teenagers. Though, they were a staple for many vacationers. Since living on the island, I'd learned how to identify a vacationer from an islander, and fanny packs were a dead giveaway. What was Matthew doing with one? Had he stolen these things? Did Blaire know she was dating a thief?

My heart plummeted into my stomach, and I actually wobbled where I stood. Too many questions were flashing through my mind.

This is what you get, I thought. This is what you get for snooping around in Blaire's life. You snooped, and now you know things you never wanted to know. Serves you right.

Upset and in desperate need of a nap, I slipped into my driver's seat and headed home.

When I pulled up to the bed and breakfast, Page and Jude were sitting on the porch swing. I'd imagined driving home and dropping the 'Blaire is dating a thief' bomb on Page immediately, not because I thought that would be best for Page, but because I was having a hard time keeping the information to myself. However, I couldn't deliver that kind of news when Jude was sitting next to her. Not only would that be an awkward conversation to have in front of a stranger, but Page would never forgive me for making her look like a fool in front of Jude. Well, she would forgive me eventually, but I knew it would be better to avoid her wrath altogether.

"Hey," I said, mounting the steps slowly, feeling like a stiff elderly person.

"Have you heard anything?" Page asked, leaning forward, her hand sliding discretely from where it had been sitting on Jude's thigh.

"About what?"

She looked at me as though I'd just spoken complete gibberish. "About the body, obviously!"

"Oh, no," I said, shrugging. "Has there been any more news?"

"You're the one who would know," she said.

Why did everyone think that? You solve a few murders and suddenly you're supposed to solve them all? I wondered if Sherlock Holmes ever felt like this. People's expectations, the pressure.

"No, I'm not," I said. "I'm just as clueless as the two of you. Also, your daughter is fine, by the way."

Page narrowed her eyes at me. "Don't try to make me feel guilty. I knew Blaire was fine as soon as you walked up. Jude told me you'd gone to check on her, and if something had been wrong, she would either be with you or you would have said it straight away."

I bit my tongue, thinking that Blaire wasn't fine, not if she was dating a thief and didn't know it.

Jude looked considerably less pale than he had earlier after we'd heard the news. "You doing okay?" I asked.

Page looked quickly between me and Jude. "Why would you not be okay?" she asked him.

He laughed an embarrassed kind of laugh and rubbed his hand across the back of his neck. "I kind of freaked out about the whole 'dead body' thing," he said. "It just surprised me."

Page leaned back on the porch swing, her hand resuming its place just above his knee. "Oh, I didn't even realize. I'm sorry."

"No, really, I'm fine," he said, waving away her concern. "You should be sorry for the dead guy, not me."

Page focused her attention back on Jude, and I left them be, deciding to talk with Page about Blaire and what I'd found in Matthew's car later.

CHAPTER 8

"That doesn't mean anything," Page said.

I stared at her, mouthing hanging open. "What do you mean it doesn't mean anything? Of course, it means something! Stolen wallets mean something, Page!"

"Would you keep your voice down?" she hissed. "Mr. and Mrs. Smith are in the room right across the hall and I don't want them to hear us in here talking about stolen wallets."

My mouth hung open. "Who even are you? How are you not concerned that your daughter might be dating a hoarder and a thief?"

"You don't know that, so I really wish you'd stop saying it as if it's a fact," Page said.

I wanted to argue more, but I also wanted to give Page time to process. I'd been stewing on the information all afternoon, and given the same amount of time, Page would certainly come to the same conclusion as I had. No normal high school boy had a stash of leather wallets and a fanny pack in his backseat without being some sort of pick pocket. There was no other explanation.

Page took my silence to mean the conversation was over, though I knew we would reopen it at a later date, and she stood up and strode over to her closet.

"I have no idea what to wear," she said.

"You didn't seem to have any issues picking out this outfit," I said, gesturing to her curve-hugging green dress and heels.

"Yeah, the problem is that this green dress is one of the nicest things I own, and I can't wear it on our date." She flipped quickly through everything in her closet and then flung her arms to her sides and stomped her foot. "Help me, Piper. You are better at this than I am."

I looked down at my own ripped boyfriend jeans and white t-shirt. "I don't see how that could be true. I'm basically a mess."

She rolled her eyes. "Don't lie to me. We both know that you work hard to look that messy."

"I'm honestly not sure whether that was a compliment or not," I said.

"It was whichever one makes you stand up and help me find something to wear."

I sighed and lifted myself off her bed. "You are so dramatic. Okay, where is he taking you?"

"A boat," she said.

I paused, waiting for her to explain further, but she stayed silent.

"I'm going to need a little more than that. Is it one of those dinner boats that circle around the shore for a few hours, or a sailboat, a speedboat, a yacht? All of those are totally different vibes and would require completely different outfits."

"I'm not sure," she said, growing suddenly exasperated. "He just said he was going to take me out on his boat."

I turned back to her closet, mouth twisted to one side of my face, deep in thought. I dug into the back, behind a multitude of identical slacks and white button downs, and pulled out a strappy black dress and threw it onto the bed next to her.

"No way," she said, picking it up by the shoulder strap and holding it as if it were a soiled pair of underwear. "This is too much. I haven't worn this in almost five years."

I ignored her and dug out a chunky white sweater, a pair of black heels, and a pair of black sneakers.

She looked at the random assortment of items unblinkingly, and then shrugged her shoulders. "Okay, you got me. I have no idea how any of these things go together."

I held up the black heels. "These will look great with that dress."

"And the sweater and the sneakers?" she asked.

I smiled, already proud of myself. "If you end up on some dinky boat in the middle of the ocean eating peanut butter and jelly sandwiches, this sweater will layer nicely over your dress and keep you warm, and these sneakers will keep you from slipping and falling into the water. You can transition perfectly from fancy night out to a casual night in with just a few pieces, both of which will fit inside of the black leather purse you have."

Page stared at me for a minute and then smiled. "Wow, you are annoyingly good at this."

"It's a gift," I said.

Page grabbed the dress and ducked into her bathroom to change, leaving the door partly open.

"I didn't know he had a boat," I said. "I thought he was just visiting the island."

"He is just visiting," Page said, grunting and breathing heavily, "but apparently he must visit fairly frequently. He stores the boat on the island."

"It must be pretty expensive to store a boat here," I said, trying to picture what Jude must do for a living. He didn't seem like a boat owner, but then again, I didn't know many boat owners. Perhaps they were all potential models. I heard several bottles tumble off the bathroom sink and clatter on the floor. "Are you okay in there?"

Rather than answer, Page pulled the door open and entered the room, her arms held out to the side like a magician after a magic trick.

I whistled. "You look amazing."

"It's not too tight?" she asked, pinching a small bit of extra fabric at her waist.

"It is, but I think that's the point," I said.

She nodded. "You're right. Also, are men still paying for dinner on first dates? I assume so, but I haven't been on a date in a while, and I'm not sure where we've landed on that particular issue with regards to feminism and equality and female empowerment."

"It's not that we don't want men to pay for us, it's that we want them to be the kind of person who would be comfortable if a woman paid for herself. If he's a gentleman, though, he should definitely pay. Especially since he's staying at our bed and breakfast for free," I said, joking.

Suddenly, Page's face tightened, nervous, and she darted back into the bathroom, closing the door behind her.

"Page?" I asked, sensing something was up almost immediately and moving to the door. "That was a joke. He has paid for his room by now, right? He said that he would have the money by today. Does he?"

She didn't answer me, so I turned the knob and pushed the door open. Page was standing in the bathroom, the dress halfway down her midsection, her raggedy tan bra showing.

"First, change into a different bra. Second, has he paid for his room or not?"

Page's shoulders stiffened and then fell. "It's just one more day. He just needs one more day, and then he can pay. It's really not a big deal," she said.

"It is a big deal," I insisted. "Especially when the business is only a few weeks old and we are still paying off renovations. We might be able to afford to make bad business decisions in the name of love later on, but at this stage, we definitely can't afford it. Everyone has to pay for their room regardless of how dreamy they are. Also, how is he taking you out on a date when he can't afford to pay for his room?"

"He'll pay tomorrow!" Page shouted, her hands clenched into fists at her sides. "I will make sure he pays tomorrow, okay? Now can we please just not talk about this? I'm already nervous enough. I don't need this dark cloud of stress hanging over my head all night."

I took a deep breath. I wasn't done lecturing Page. She had given me so many long, drawn out lectures over the years that it was nice to finally have the opportunity to dish it back. However, it was clear she was nervous. She hadn't been on a first date in almost twenty years, and she was excited. I finally had the sister I saw in all of the movies. The one who wanted to talk about guys and who I helped get ready for dates. It was weird for us, but nice, and I didn't want to ruin it.

"We can put a pin in it," I said, pointing at her with a serious finger. "But we will reconvene tomorrow if the issue hasn't been dealt with."

Page rolled her eyes, but then gave me an appreciative smile. "Thanks, Piper."

"What are sisters for?" I said.

I turned, pulled open her top drawer, and tossed her a black strapless bra. "But seriously, take off that granny bra. Even if Jude can't see it, he'll sense it. It's so old it's probably haunted."

~

I was sitting on the sitting room couch reading one of the trashy romance novels Page had begged me to throw out and not display on our library shelves, but that I'd instead expertly hidden behind her many legal dramas, when I heard Blaire walk through the front door.

"Hey, B," I said, setting the open book face down across my knee.

Blaire turned the corner into the sitting room and I immediately forgot all about the particularly steamy scene I'd been reading, and let the book fall to the floor. "What's going on? What's wrong?"

Her face was as pale as printer paper against her dark black hair, and her lower lip was bright red from chewing on it, something she only did when she was upset. During her parents' divorce, her lip had been permanently cracked and bleeding.

"I saw a picture of the dead body," she said, still standing in the doorway as though she were rooted to the spot.

"What? How?" I asked, growing angry. I'd seen too many dead bodies for a lifetime in the past few months, and it was shocking every time. I'd prayed Blaire would never have to see anything like that. "Did Shep show you? I'll kill him," I said, reaching for my cell phone, already reciting the police station number in my head.

She shook her head. "No, he didn't. He showed Matthew's parents, but Greg held the picture up to Matthew to see if he recognized him, and I caught a glimpse."

"That old drunk," I said, still grabbing my phone. I didn't know Greg's number, but I'd find it out and give him a piece of my mind. The island was small enough that everyone knew everyone else's business, addresses and phone numbers included. "You and Matthew shouldn't have even been there for that. What were they thinking?"

"I'm not a child, Aunt Piper!" Blaire said, nearly shouting.

"I know, Blaire, it's just—"

She interrupted me. "Would you listen to me for a second?"

I bit my tongue, took a deep breath, and nodded.

"I'm not upset because I saw a dead body. I've seen worse things in movies than that photo. I'm upset because I saw the picture, and I recognized the man."

My heart dropped. I hadn't even considered that. The dead person wasn't found on our property, so I'd assumed it had nothing to do with us, but I hadn't paused for a minute to think about *who* the dead person could be. Had I become so accustomed to dead bodies lying around that I'd forgotten they were once real people?

"Who was it?" I asked, my voice coming out in a whisper, though I didn't know why.

"The guy," she said.

My serious face fell away and my eyes narrowed. "Oh, you mean the guy from the place? Come on, Blaire, that is zero information. I need more than that."

"Sorry," she said, shaking her head. "The guy from the other day. The one mom sent away for not being able to pay for his room."

"Oh, okay," I said, trying to decide if that had anything to do with us or the house or the bed and breakfast. "Well, that's not great, but technically he never even stayed here, so his death still has nothing to do with us."

"Is that seriously what you're worried about, Aunt Piper?" Blaire asked. "Whether or not it will hurt business?"

"Well, kind of," I said, glancing at the floor, embarrassed to have come off so callous in front of Blaire. "But, I mean, obviously it's too bad what happened to him."

"Too bad?" Blaire asked, her eyebrows raised almost to her hairline. "He was bashed in the head. I saw his brains."

"I get it, Blaire. I'm sorry. Obviously, it's terrible. And I'm sorry you had to see that. You know I understand how that feels, and I would never wish that sight on anyone, but I don't know what else you want me to say."

Blaire stared at me, her eyes deep and pensive. Then, she shrugged her shoulders and turned away, heading for the stairs. "Nothing, never mind. I don't expect you to say anything. Nothing is wrong, and I'm fine."

"Blare, wait," I said, calling after her, trying to understand what I'd done wrong.

"Goodnight," she yelled down the stairs. I heard her moving down the long hallway to her room, the old floors creaking with every step, and then her door slammed shut.

CHAPTER 9

The next morning found me, once again, handling breakfast by myself. I'd heard Page come home extremely late
the night before, so I hadn't even bothered trying to wake
her. And from what little I'd gathered from Blaire's
behavior the night before, I'd done something horribly
wrong, and she was quite angry with me.

"You're a regular Rachael Ray."

I turned to see Jude standing in the kitchen doorway,
his hair still wet from a shower and sticking straight up,
as though he'd just run a towel through his hair and come
downstairs. Men were so annoying. They didn't even have
to try and they looked great.

"Or, is that sexist?" he asked, his eyes widening, but a
smile still sitting on his lips. "Should I call you Gordon
Ramsey or Emeril, instead?"

I laughed. "Absolutely not. Rachael Ray is preferable.
How was your night?"

I asked because I was desperate to know about his date

with Page, but I also thought Page might appreciate hearing how things were from his point of view. Of course, if he'd had a terrible time, he probably wouldn't tell me, but perhaps I'd be able to discover something from his phrasing or his body language.

"Great," he said, reaching for a banana on the island and peeling it back. "It was a lot of fun."

Well, that was effectively useless information. No detail and too few words to over analyze with Page later. I flipped the three pancakes cooking on the griddle and then turned back to him, trying to put the pressure on. "I heard Page come home pretty late," I said.

He shrugged. "Not too late, though I suppose that depends on your definition."

"After midnight is late by every definition," I joked.

His eyes narrowed. "I didn't think it was that late when we got back."

"You must have had so much fun you lost track of time," I said.

Jude turned his head to the side as though he were trying to remember something, and then he shrugged it off and smiled at me. "I suppose so. Well, I'll leave you to it. Mr. and Mrs. Smith looked extra hungry this morning, so you have a lot of pancakes to make."

He wasn't lying. Mr. Smith ate a stack of four pancakes, squirting a huge dollop of syrup between each one, and Mrs. Smith had three. I had to make more pancakes halfway through breakfast to keep up with them.

When Page finally came downstairs, I was loading the dishwasher.

"There's our little party girl," I said. "Good morning."

Page yawned and smoothed down her shirt. She'd gone back to her usual wardrobe of black slacks and a white button down. "Good morning. Sorry I missed breakfast. I slept through my alarm."

"That's alright. You just owe me a super huge massive favor," I said.

Page groaned. "You're going to ask me to clean the bathrooms, aren't you?"

"For a week," I said, smiling.

"Three days," she bartered.

"Four!"

She grabbed her box of bran cereal from the cupboard and poured a bowl. "Fine, but you still have to empty the trash cans. The trash cans are the responsibility of the person on trash duty, not the person on bathroom duty."

"Deal," I said, thrilled at the thought of going four days without cleaning splatter stains off of toilet lids. "Have you talked to Blaire yet?"

Page shook her head. "No, her door was closed and the light was off. I guess she's still sleeping. Why?"

I explained our brief conversation the night before, and how she'd stormed off to her room.

"Wait, the guy I was talking to? The guy who threatened to sue us?" Page asked, face pale, her mouth hanging open.

I nodded. "That's what she said."

"This is not good. Not good at all," she mumbled, stirring her cereal absently, the bran flakes disintegrating into milky sludge. "We cannot have another death on our hands."

"It's not on our hands," I said. "He didn't even stay the night here."

"Right! Because I turned him away! He may have lived if I'd let him stay."

"Page, that is ridiculous," I said. Though, honestly, I had to admit she had a point. He died that very night. If he'd stayed at the bed and breakfast, he likely would have spent the evening playing board games and losing to Mrs. Smith, who seemed to always win, despite the games being entirely luck based.

I could see Page spiraling away into guilt and I tried to bring her back.

"The only person responsible is the person who bashed in his head," I said.

"His head was bashed in?"

I nodded. "And your daughter saw a picture of it."

"Oh, Blaire is fine," Page said, waving away my concern. "Remember how badly she wanted to go down to the beach to see the body you found buried in the sand? This kind of stuff doesn't bother her."

"I'm not so sure. She seemed really upset."

"Welcome to living with a teenager," she said, spreading her arms wide as though she were a particular movie character beckoning me in to a fantastical chocolate factory. All she needed was a purple top hat and a cane. "She could have been upset about a million other things, but just chose to channel it into that for the moment. One time she was upset because she spilled coffee all over her favorite shirt, and she screamed at me for not using my blinker while I was driving home."

"That makes sense, though. It's super annoying when

people don't use their blinker," I said. "Honestly, it is just a tiny flick of the wrist and the whole road is a much safer place. You should use your blinker."

Page rolled her eyes. "The point is that Blaire is rarely ever actually mad about what it seems like she is mad about. There are layers to her. Like an onion."

"That is a stupid saying. When you peel back a layer of an onion, you know what you find? More onion. It's just more of the same. You should really say that she is like a jaw breaker. At least those layers are different colors."

"Either way, you know what I mean," she said, finally taking a bite of her cereal and grimacing. It had gone entirely soggy. She pushed it away and picked up a muffin. "Do you think we should reach out to Shep?"

"About what?" I asked.

"The guy. The dead guy. He was here earlier that day. They might want our insights to help figure out the timeline. Isn't that something they like to figure out when someone turns up dead? The timeline?"

"Yeah, I suppose so. It wouldn't hurt to reach out. I'll give him a call once I'm finished in here." I wedged the last plate into the dishwasher between a frying pan covered in egg remnants and several glasses with chocolate milk residue around the top. "I saw your boyfriend this morning. He said your date was 'great.'"

"Did he?" Page asked, trying to look nonchalant, but unable to contain her smile. Then, realizing what I had said, she bit down the corner of her mouth. "He isn't my boyfriend."

I nodded. "Was it a great date for you, too?"

"He packed a picnic basket with cheese and bread and

wine, and we listened to jazz music on a tiny portable radio while we looked at the stars. It was totally cheesy, like a scene from a movie," she said.

"So, you absolutely loved it?"

"Totally," she gushed. "It was the most romantic thing ever. And I pulled out my chunky sweater and sneakers halfway through the night when it got chilly."

"You're welcome," I said.

Page tipped her head to me in recognition of my help, and then stood up, brushing the crumbs from her muffin off the table and into her palm. "I should go check on Blaire and make sure everything is okay. But you'll call Shep this morning?"

"I'll do it right now."

"Thanks," she said. "I'm ready to put this whole thing behind us."

Putting it behind us would prove slightly more difficult than having a simple conversation with Shep. In the time between Page going upstairs and my call to Shep, three different guests came into the kitchen to ask me about the dead body that had been found on the beach. Somehow, the rumor mill on Sunrise Island had already begun to turn, and people knew that he'd been at the bed and breakfast earlier in the day. The guests were concerned about what may have motivated someone to kill the man, and whether it had anything to do with the bed and breakfast. I tried to remind them all that the island was small and the man had likely been to many local hangouts before his death, and that his brief appearance at the bed and breakfast had nothing to do with his death. However, people were hardly convinced.

When I finally called Shep, he answered on the second ring. "I was wondering when you'd be calling."

"I gather you've made the connection between the dead guy and the bed and breakfast?"

There was a long pause. "What?"

"The murder investigation...the man was at the bed and breakfast earlier in the day," I said, my words drawn out in a kind of question.

"Oh, well, no," Shep said, clearing his throat. "I thought you were calling to assist with the investigation."

Even our out of town guests were buzzing with the news that the deceased had spent one of his last moments on our property. How did the sheriff not know about it yet? Also, how was he still convinced I was going to help with his investigation? I'd declined his offer in no uncertain terms. What did it say about our police force that he was sitting in his office waiting for me to call rather than out chasing leads?

"I suppose I am helping in a way," I said. "Page and I want to come in and give you everything we know."

"You two are offering to come in and be interviewed?" he asked. "That's unusual."

"We aren't turning ourselves in or anything," I said, making sure that was incredibly clear, because with Shep, you never really knew. "We just know there must be an ongoing investigation and we wanted to offer up what little information we have."

He took a long time to respond, but finally said, "How about today at 3?"

"See you then, Shep."

I hung up and closed my eyes, doubting my decision to move to Sunrise Island. Sure, it had scenic views and the near-constant humidity meant my hair never went staticky, but how safe did I really feel? Not only had I become a target of two different murderers, but the police force didn't seem to have a handle on things. Especially since the police force was Shep and a few brainless deputies. I shook my head and pushed myself to a standing position. It didn't matter. This murder investigation wasn't my business. Page and I were going to give Shep an interview and then I was going to mind my own business. Shep didn't need my help. Or, at least, he shouldn't need my help, and I certainly didn't want him to get used to having it. So, no, I absolutely was not going to work on this investigation.

I repeated that to myself several times throughout the afternoon as my mind wandered back to thoughts of the dead man. *I am not going to help with this investigation.*

CHAPTER 10

"Thanks for coming in," Shep said, meeting us in the front lobby of the tiny jail house.

The place had a small lobby with tan tile floors, dingy white walls, a large receptionist's desk that appeared to be empty, and three metal chairs in a waiting area. Through a large pane of glass in the back wall I could see into the holding cell. It was a large room with a wall of bars cutting it in half, forming one large cell.

"Of course," Page said. "Anything we can do to help."

I could tell she was nervous, and I wanted to whisper to Page that she didn't need to be so professional—Shep was barely holding it together—but I held my tongue and followed them both through a side door, which led to a wood-panelled office.

"Take a seat," Shep said, gesturing to two chairs across from a cluttered desk. One was a wooden arm chair, the other a plastic lawn chair. "I only had the one chair, so please forgive the lawn chair. I brought it from my patio at home."

"No problem at all," Page said, beaming her brightest smile at him as she sat in the wooden chair.

I shot her a look as I lowered myself into the plastic chair, but she either didn't notice or ignored it.

"So how does this work?" she asked. "Is there a recorder somewhere or are you just going to write it down, or…?"

Shep looked at her blankly. "I was just going to listen to what you had to say."

Page hesitated, her mouth partially open in surprise, and then she nodded. "Right, of course. That works."

She turned to me with a wary look in her eyes, but I just smiled. I hadn't expected anything more from Shep, but clearly Page had expected something more along the lines of the many detective shows we'd watched growing up.

"So, you knew the deceased?" Shep asked, folding his hands carefully on the desk in front of him, leaning forward onto his elbows.

Page nodded. "Well, we didn't *know* him. But we briefly encountered him."

"He tried to book a room at the bed and breakfast," I said.

"Tried?" Shep asked.

"His payment didn't go through," Page said. "He asked if we could let him stay in a room until he sorted out whatever was wrong with his bank account, but I told him we couldn't, and he got upset."

I shook my head. "He was more than upset. He became disorderly and threatening."

"He threatened you?" Shep asked, perking up as if he would jump up and go arrest whoever had disrespected us, even though that person was now sitting in the morgue.

"He threatened the business," Page said. "He swore to write a bad review and warn people against booking with us."

"And did he?" Shep asked.

Page and I looked at one another and then turned to Shep at the same time, wondering how to tell him without making him seem stupid.

"No, he didn't," I said. "He died…"

He just looked at us both and nodded, his facial expression not changing except for one single twitch of his mustache. "And then what happened?"

"He drove off," I said. "He took off in his red rental car and we didn't see him again."

"He didn't come back by the bed and breakfast later in the day or call you?" Shep asked.

Page shook her head. "No, we didn't hear or see anything about him until my daughter told me she recognized him as the guy I'd argued with."

"Katie over at the General Store had some guy come in late that same night who asked if she could float him some cigarettes and then made a phone call. You might talk to her," I said.

Shep nodded and for the first time since we'd sat down, reached for his pen and wrote down 'KATIE' in large block letters on the back of what appeared to be an old receipt.

"Is there anything else you can tell me?" he asked.

We told him no, and he walked us to the front door.

"If you think of anything else, be sure to let me know," he said. "Have a good one."

When we got back in the car, Page was sweating.

"I am so glad that's over," she said, wiping her palms on the back of her jeans.

I started the car and reversed onto the empty road. "It wasn't even a big deal. We just offered up some basic information."

"No." Page shook her head. "We put ourselves on the radar. I can feel it. He totally suspects us."

I laughed. "Shep wouldn't suspect us if we showed up with the dead man's wallet and blood on our hands. He's clueless."

"You don't give him enough credit," Page said.

"For the sake of the dead man and his family, I hope you're right," I said. "I hope he can find out who did this. But based on how desperate he was to get me on the case, I highly doubt he has any leads."

"He wanted you to help him with the case?" she asked, turning to me, mouth hanging open.

"He's asked twice now."

"Are you going to do it?" Page asked.

I glanced at her several times, trying to decide if she was being serious. "Is this a joke or am I supposed to answer?"

"Why would it be a joke?" she asked.

I lost it. "Because you have been livid at me both times

I've investigated a murder on this island. Why would I do it again?"

"This time is different," she said. "We may have been the last people to see him alive. That doesn't look good."

"No, Katie was the last person to see him alive," I corrected her.

"You don't know that. She hasn't positively identified him yet, has she? For all we know, he left our bed and breakfast and was dead five minutes later."

Page stared out the window and I shook my head, disbelieving. This was the first time when the dead body had almost nothing to do with us or our business or our property, and now Page wanted me to get involved. Whereas, when the dead body was dug up on our property, I was supposed to stay out of it. How was a girl supposed to keep up with wonky rules like that?

Finally, Page broke the silence. "All I'm saying is that if Shep can't solve this, you should help. We want this case closed as soon as possible so no speculation lands on us."

I wanted to argue further and convince Page she was being irrational, that no blame would ever land on us because we were entirely innocent, but instead I swallowed my words, gripped the steering wheel tighter, and nodded my head in agreement. "Fine. If Shep can't do it, I'll help."

"Thanks, Piper."

My knuckles turned white as I turned off of Main Street and onto the long dirt road that led to the B&B. Shep needed to get his crap together and figure the case out, because I was not in the mood to solve another murder.

~

The first thing we heard upon entering the house was Blaire crying.

"Blaire?" Page asked, shooting a worried look at me and then following the sound of her daughter's sobs into the sitting room.

Blaire was huddled on the couch, and Mrs. Smith had her arm around her shaking shoulders, whispering comforts into her ear.

"It will be all right, sweetie. These things have a way of working out in the end."

Blaire shook her head and released another series of loud sobs and hiccups.

"What is going on?" Page asked.

Mrs. Smith stood up and Page took her spot, gently touching the old woman on the shoulder in silent thanks.

"Blaire, honey, what's the matter?" she asked, leaning forward and trying to look into her daughter's face.

Blaire shook her head.

"She wouldn't tell me what was the matter," Mrs. Smith whispered to me, shrugging her shoulders. "I found her all doubled over on the couch, and I couldn't just leave her there alone."

"I'm so sorry about this," I said, suddenly rethinking my decision to move myself and my family into the same house we ran our business out of. Moments like this were certain to happen more often than not, especially with a teenager in the house.

Mrs. Smith waved me away and smiled. "I have two daughters. Of course, they are grown and gone now with children of their own, but the mothering instinct never really leaves you. I remember their teenage years like it was yesterday. It can be such a hard time."

Mrs. Smith shuffled down the hallway to, no doubt, join Mr. Smith in the backyard. He'd been spending most afternoons reading on the bench under the large oak tree. I made a mental note to not begrudge them their morning pancakes, and give Mr. Smith as much syrup as his plate could hold.

I turned to find Blaire in a slightly more upright position, Page drawing the information out of her in between sobs.

"Something about Matthew?" Page asked, her face contorted into concern, though she didn't know for what yet.

Blaire nodded. "He's in trouble."

"Like, grounded?"

Blaire shook her head.

"Honey, you have to stop crying and tell me what is going on," Page said gently.

"With Shep," Blaire blubbered. "He's in trouble with Shep."

"What did he do?"

She sucked in a few shaky breaths, and then, seeming to calm herself, explained.

"The dead man didn't have a wallet, and the police were searching for it. They suspected it could have been a burglary gone bad. Well, while they were searching the marina, they found a stash of wallets in the back of Matthew's car."

I shot Page an 'I told you so' look, and she rolled her

eyes. Now clearly wasn't the time to rub my rightness in her face, but it sure did feel good. Blaire, thankfully, didn't seem to notice.

"Shep asked if he could search his car, and Matthew agreed, and Shep recognized some of the names on the wallets. People had reported them missing."

"Matthew stole them?" Page asked, trying to hide her severe disapproval in favor of getting the facts.

"No, Mom. No," Blaire said, shaking her head fiercely. "He never stole them from anyone. They were delivered to the lost and found, and when no one came to claim them in a few days, he would take the cash out of them and keep them. It wasn't a big deal."

Page hesitated, and when she spoke, her voice was uncharacteristically gentle. "Blaire, that is stealing. Those wallets should have been returned to their owners, money included."

"He makes almost nothing working at the marina, even though his parents own it, and those people who store boats there are loaded anyway. They won't miss twenty dollars. It wasn't a big deal."

"If it isn't a big deal, then why are you crying?" Page asked. I could tell she was saving this argument for another time. Regardless of what Blaire thought, Matthew was stealing, and that was not a desirable trait for your daughter's boyfriend to possess.

"It isn't a big deal, but now Shep thinks that maybe Matthew has the dead guy's wallet," Blaire said. When neither Page nor I seemed to react the way she expected, Blaire continued. "He thinks Matthew may have robbed the guy."

Still, Page and I stared at her, trying to understand why she was weeping.

"They think Matthew killed him!" Blaire finally said in a frustrated scream, the words sending her into another burst of sobbing.

CHAPTER 11

"That's ridiculous," Page said, stroking Blaire's hair. "They can't possibly think a teenager could kill a man just because he was caught nicking a few wallets from the lost and found. They'll interview him and he will give his alibi, and it will all be fine."

After seeing the wallets in Matthew's backseat, I'd thought the worst, but the worst for me had been that he was a run of the mill pick pocket. He couldn't be a murderer, could he?

"Right," I said, agreeing with Page and moving to sit on the other side of Blaire. "You two are together constantly. What were you up to the night of the murder?"

Blaire's eyes rolled back as she thought, her mind replaying the last few days, and then they shot wide. "We weren't together."

This revelation sent her into another bout of sobbing. She leaned forward and folded her arms on her knees, burying her face in them.

"He will be fine, Blaire. Really," Page said, massaging Blaire's back.

"I'll call Shep," I said. "He'll tell me what is going on and I'm sure they've already let Matthew go."

I moved into the entryway and dialed Shep's number, my annoyance level rising with every unanswered ring. Finally, after nearly ten rings, Shep picked up.

"Sunrise Island Police Department, Sheriff speaking," he said, his voice drawling out around the vowels.

"You didn't think it was pertinent to let me know that my niece's boyfriend was a suspect in the case?" I said, skipping any sort of introduction.

There was a pause. "Who is this?"

"Who do you think it is, Shep?" There was no way he didn't recognize my voice by now. Or my number, for that matter. I'd called him too many times for him to play dumb.

"It wasn't any of your business, Piper. You said you didn't want to help with the investigation."

"I don't want to *work* the investigation," I said. "There is a difference. You could have told me someone close to me was a suspect so I could try and clear their name."

"I didn't realize Matthew was close to you, and I'm the Sheriff. I'm the one who clears people," Shep said, sounding exhausted. "You gave me what little information you had, and I'm grateful, but if you aren't going to assist on the case, then I'm afraid I really must be going. Lots to do here."

"Like wrongfully arrest teenagers?" I shot back.

He sighed. "Goodbye, Piper."

I hung up feeling useless. It was unusual being on the

other side of the investigations. Although I didn't want to put myself in the middle of yet another murder case, I also liked knowing what was going on. I liked being in front of the island gossip, and it would be a large adjustment learning about the latest developments from the mailman or Katie when I picked something up from the General Store.

"What did he say?" Page asked, poking her head out of the sitting room.

I shrugged. "Nothing, really. He basically told me not to bother him."

"Dang it. I was hoping you'd have something to make Blaire feel better. She is certain Matthew is going to be charged with murder, and I can't seem to convince her otherwise."

"It will all blow over, though. They'll find a new lead and forget about Matthew," I said.

Page nodded. "I know, but that doesn't help me right now. I'm supposed to meet Jude at the Marina for another date, but I can't leave Blaire like this."

"Another date?" I wagged my eyebrows at her flirtatiously. "You two are pretty serious."

Page blushed, but otherwise ignored me. "It doesn't matter if my daughter is a sobbing mess."

I waved away her concern. "I'll be here, and who knows how long Jude will be in town. You have to make the most of it while you can."

"Are you sure?" Page asked, looking over her shoulder at the shaking ball that was her daughter and then back to me, her eyes wary.

"I've been babysitting Blaire since she was a baby. She

used to cry over a poopy diaper and now she cries over her boyfriend being arrested. It's new, but it's nothing I can't handle."

"Are you sure?"

I rolled my eyes. "You already asked me that. Yes, I'm sure. Absolutely positive. I've got this. Go on your date."

Page's face lit up. "Okay! I'll tell Blaire goodbye and then I've got to get going. I'm going to be ten minutes late as it is."

"Hurry," I said, shooing her along. "We'll be fine."

By the time Page said goodbye to Blaire, changed into jeans and a flowy white blouse, and reversed down the driveway, Blaire was sitting up on the couch and crying. Sure, she was still upset, but at least she was vertical. Progress.

The rest of the evening was spent watching anything on tv that didn't remind Blaire of murder or violence or romance, which left us with the Golf channel and QVC. We spent half an hour being sold birthstone rings that were buy one get one half off, which made no sense to me since people only have one birthday. They would either have to buy two rings with the same birthstone or buy one for themselves and one for someone else. I brought this point up to Blaire, but she seemed to ignore me.

Mason called me once and asked if I was free, but I explained the situation with Matthew and Blaire and we agreed to try and see each other another night. He had no interest in spending his evening with an emotional teenage girl. More and more it felt as though we'd never find time to hang out again. Something always came up.

Headlights moved up the driveway, splashing through

the window and dousing the dark sitting room in glaring light. Blaire rolled over and covered her eyes as though she were a vampire. I looked through the window and saw Page's car.

"It's your mom," I said, patting her leg. "At least sit up so she doesn't think I just sat here and let you veg on television all night."

"But you did let me sit here and veg on television all night," Blaire said.

I hit her leg a bit harder. "But your mother doesn't need to know that. Sit up!"

Blaire had reluctantly lifted herself to a half-reclined position by the time Page unlocked and opened the front door, which I figured was good enough.

"How was the date?" I glanced at the clock and saw that it was only 8 PM. "It didn't last long."

"It didn't last at all," she said, shoving her keys into her purse and roughly snapping it closed.

"What do you mean?"

"He stood me up!" Page shouted.

Suddenly full of energy, Blaire sat up, her eyes narrowed. "How could he have stood you up? Isn't he staying at our bed and breakfast?"

"I don't know anymore. His car isn't in the lot and he isn't answering his phone." Page shrugged and flopped down onto the couch next to Blaire. "I sat on his boat for an hour and a half just hoping he'd show up with some magnificent excuse. I feel like such an idiot."

"No," I said, shaking my head. "He should feel like the idiot. He stood up a magnificent woman. He is the one who should feel stupid, not you."

Page lowered her head, her dark hair spilling over her eyes. "He never paid for his room. He was probably only using me to get a few nights for free before he bailed. I doubt he ever even liked me. It didn't make any sense anyway."

"That guy is worthless," Blaire said, her outrage making her momentarily forget about her own relationship problems. "He wasn't even that handsome."

Page grimaced and nodded weakly, but I could tell she didn't really agree with her daughter, she was just trying to put on a brave face.

"Blaire," I said. "Why don't you go make some tea."

"Tea?" she asked, eyebrows raised. "Are we grandmas? What about coffee?"

"Decaf," I said.

Blaire winked at me and trotted off to the kitchen.

"There has to be an explanation," I said, dragging Page to the couch by the arm. "He was totally into you."

Page rolled her eyes, and now that I was closer, I could tell she'd been crying. I was going to punch Jude square in the face next time I saw him. I could count on one hand the number of times I'd seen Page cry, so he had seriously hurt her. "He was totally into the idea of getting a few nights in a nice bed and breakfast for free. I was scammed."

"You two already went on one date," I reminded her. "Why would he have done that if he wasn't interested at all?"

"To string me along! To buy himself some extra time to finish his business and get out," she suggested.

Clearly Page was too emotional to think rationally.

This wouldn't be sorted out until we tracked down Jude and confronted him.

"What was his business on the island, anyway?" I asked. "He never really made it clear."

Page shook her head, her eyebrows furrowing. "I don't think he said...oh no..."

"What?" I asked, a nervous energy tingling up my spine.

"He didn't give me any personal details about himself. He let me do all of the talking. Every time I asked him a personal question he would deflect and turn the conversation towards me," she said, her voice high and flustered. "I didn't manage to learn a single detail about him aside from his name."

"If Jude Lawton is his real name," I said, half-joking.

Page, however, didn't find it very funny. "Do you think he lied about his name, too?"

I held up my hands. "Okay, slow down. I was joking. I'm sure he told you his real name, and I'm sure it isn't a big deal that he didn't talk about his business."

"Does Texas have a mafia? You always hear about the mafia in New York and Los Angeles, but the mafia is everywhere, right?"

"He's not in the mafia, Page! Get a grip."

"You are usually the one with theories and suspicions, Piper! Why not now? Why are you defending him?"

The truth was, the more I thought about Jude and his actions over the past few days, certain things did stand out. However, my relationship with Page had always been about balance, and now that she was diving off the deep end, it was my job to stand on the edge and secure her harness so she didn't tumble into the void. I couldn't follow her or we'd both be lost in a sea of unprovable theories and accusations. One of us had to remain on dry land, and in this moment, that person was me.

I sat my hand on Page's knee and squeezed. "I'm not defending that jerk," I said, looking her square in the face so she could see how serious I was. "I just think we need to wait until we have all of the facts. I'm sure we will see him tomorrow and he'll be able to explain everything. And if he can't, I'll kick him in the crotch."

Page released a choked laugh, and I saw the panic leave her eyes. She looked like herself again, rational and steady, like a flag pole rather than the flag.

We sat up until late in the night, talking, and though Page never admitted it, I knew it was because she was waiting for Jude to show up. I couldn't blame her. I'd been stood up on a blind date once, and I spent the next several days staring into the eyes of every man I passed wondering whether it was him. Love can make you crazy, and Blaire and Page were great examples of that. It was almost laughable to think that I'd been despairing over my relationship with Mason. My love life was a breeze compared to theirs. Perhaps I should have forced Mason to come over to the house and hang out. That way he could have had a front row seat to the chaos, and left feeling much more confident in our relationship.

When Page went to sleep, I broke our policy and unlocked Jude's door, ignoring the 'Do Not Disturb' sign hanging on the door. I didn't go all the way in, but I poked my head around the door and saw his duffel bag sitting neatly at the foot of the bed, which was enough for me.

Unless he planned to leave all of his clothes behind, he'd be back. And when he showed up, I'd have a few choice words for him.

~

Page was jumpy all of the next morning. She woke up before me and started breakfast, despite having no idea what was on the menu. When I got down to the kitchen, she had started making everything in the pantry—muffins, bagels, toast, pancakes, eggs, biscuits and gravy. The counters were strewn with every baking dish, pan, and utensil we owned, and I immediately knew I'd be running to the General Store to stock up on everything in the next day or two. We didn't have another bulk shipment coming for three days, and Page had used up almost all of our eggs. Swallowing my annoyance, I took a deep breath and kept my mouth shut.

"You've been busy," I said, making myself a cup of coffee. If I was going to keep up with Page, I was going to need at least two cups.

She jumped and turned to me, wide-eyed. Upon realizing it was me, she settled. "I couldn't sleep, and you've done breakfast all of this week. It was my turn."

"I do breakfast every day," I corrected her. Sure, Page usually helped, but I was the cook. Page had been married for sixteen years, but she'd never been the stereotypical homemaker. They'd lived on boxed meals and the recipes from a cookbook I'd bought her called 'Three-Ingredient Recipes for the Busy Mom.'

"Well, I'm doing it today," she snapped. And then,

taking a deep breath, "I'm sorry. I didn't sleep much last night."

"So you said." I downed half off my mug, feeling the coffee scald the roof of my mouth, and refilled it. "Any sign of Jude?"

She shrugged. "I haven't checked."

We both knew she was lying, but I didn't want to be the one to point it out. She'd been up so early waiting for him. I knew it, she knew it. I bet Mrs. Harris knew it, even though she hadn't left the attic in a few days.

"Screw him," I said.

Page smiled, and we finished breakfast in a companionable silence.

Taking the plates out to the dining room was a different story. Page went through the door just before me—a serving tray of scrambled eggs in one hand, a stack of pancakes in the other—but she came to a dead stop as soon as the door opened. She stopped so suddenly I nearly plowed into her, only a miracle saving the toast, biscuits, and bowl of gravy I was carrying.

"Wha—" I started, but then I saw him.

Jude was sitting at the head of the table, in the same spot he'd occupied the last few mornings, as if nothing had changed.

"That son of a—"

"Good morning, everyone," Page said, a smile in her voice. She sounded like a cartoon princess, happy and sing-songy. Whereas I was still standing halfway between the kitchen and the dining room, fuming.

When Jude saw Page waltzing around the room, his face dropped into a mask of concern, but Page didn't even look at him. She delivered the plates to the table and then wiggled past me to go into the kitchen for more plates. I dropped back into the kitchen after her.

"What are you going to do?" I whispered.

"About what?" she asked.

"Jude!" I nearly shouted, and then lowered my voice. "About Jude."

Page's face remained neutral. "Nothing."

"Nothing?"

Page nodded, loaded up her arms with more plates, and walked back through the swinging door and disappeared into the dining room

Compared to last night, this Page was a Buddhist monk. She was totally zen. I shrugged my shoulders and followed her.

Though Page didn't even glance in Jude's direction, his eyes followed her around the room, and I could tell he was begging her to look his direction. Finally, after Page refused to see him, he looked at me. I was caught off guard and glanced away quickly, but it was too late. His eyes had asked me to understand, to give him a chance to explain, and I'd seen it. I'd been prepared to walk into the room and hate him. To kick him in the crotch like I'd promised Page, but now I knew I'd have to hear him out. I moved towards his end of the table to deliver my plates, and Jude took his opportunity.

"My phone died," he whispered to me, grabbing a slice of toast from the plate I set in front of him. "I had to go back to the mainland for some business and I thought I'd be back in time, but I got held up, and my phone died, and I didn't have Page's number memorized."

Dang it. He had a good excuse.

"Do you think she'll talk to me?" he asked. "Can I fix it?"

I looked at Page. She was focused on Mrs. Smith, talking about the new jet skis they'd just purchased on a whim the day before. I made a mental note to find out what kind of business they'd been in before retirement. Whatever it was, it had been lucrative.

I shrugged. "I'll see what I can do."

When we got back to the kitchen, Page turned on me the moment the door closed.

"Why were you talking to him?" she fumed, her eyes red-rimmed. "You weren't supposed to talk to him!"

I was taken aback, surprised. The last time we'd been alone in the kitchen, Page had seemed fine, if a little tense. Now, though, she was unhinged.

"First of all, he's a guest. Am I supposed to not speak with our guests? Second of all, you never said I couldn't talk to him."

"It was implied, Piper," Page said, her annoyance making her look remarkably like Blaire. "What did he say?"

I relayed the conversation to her, and then waited.

Finally, Page shook her head. "He could have called the bed and breakfast number. That's searchable on the internet, and one of us would have answered. He could have left a message."

I hadn't thought of that. Though, that also meant that perhaps Jude hadn't thought of it, either. I voiced this possibility to Page, but she didn't seem eager to hear it or forgive him.

"If it helps, he looked longingly at you the entire time he was talking," I said.

"Of course, he did," Page said, flipping her dark hair over her shoulder. "I'm a catch."

I laughed, and Page did, too. Then she rolled her eyes. "Is it bad that I really want to go back out there and talk to him?"

"It's only bad if you think it's bad," I said. "I can't tell you what to do."

"But what would you do?" she asked.

Page rarely asked my opinion on anything. I'd always been the one going to her for advice, so this was a new experience, and I didn't want to screw up.

"Well, not to be blunt, but you don't have a lot of other dating options," I said, ignoring the dirty look she shot me. "You might as well see this relationship through to its fiery end. And who knows? Maybe this was just a huge mix-up and things will be great and Blaire will have a stepdad."

Page scrunched up her nose and was preparing to respond when the doorbell rang and interrupted her train of thought.

"I'll get it," she said.

She darted out of the kitchen, but curiosity got the better of me and I followed her to the door. The sun was just beginning to burn away the early morning dew, and pockets of fog still hung heavily on the horizon. It was too early for anyone we knew to be coming by, and we didn't have any new guests checking in for two days.

Page pulled the door open, and revealed Shep standing on the porch, his hand resting dangerously close to the gun holstered on his hip. He never carried a gun. Every time I'd ever seen him, the holster was empty.

"Good morning, Shep," Page said, smiling and then standing aside to invite him in.

Shep shook his head, and I suddenly realized how tense he was. He looked like Blaire at her sixth-grade spelling bee right before she threw up all over the stage.

"What's going on?" I asked, moving into the entryway. Something felt off, but I couldn't put my finger on it. Perhaps it was about my phone call to Shep the night before. Maybe he felt like he had to make a house call to come and put me in my place, remind me that he was the sheriff and I was a citizen. That I had no right to call him and interfere with his investigation. If that was the case, I was prepared to remind him that he'd begged me, not once, but *twice* to assist him with the investigation and that offered me every right to tell him when he was barking up the wrong tree.

I heard someone tumbling down the stairs and I turned to see Blaire standing there, her eyes nearly swollen shut, still in her pajamas.

"Is it about Matthew?" she asked. "Is he still in custody?"

Shep shook his head. "We released him this morning."

I sighed. So that's why he'd come. To apologize. To thank me for sending him along to Katie who probably offered up a clue that led him down a different path.

"Thanks for letting us know," I said. "You could have just called."

Shep's face fell into an unknowable expression, his mouth tense.

"Page Lane," he said. "I'm going to need you to come down to the station with me. I have a few questions."

"Okay?" Page said, her voice a question.

"No, wait," I said, feeling the tension in the air. "What's this about?"

Shep looked more professional than usual and he was repeating lines from cop shows.

"It's fine, Piper. He just wants to ask me some questions," Page said, smiling apologetically at Shep.

Shep looked at me and then lowered his eyes to the ground and I knew. He didn't even need to say it.

"No, Page," I said, shaking my head, keeping my voice low. Several of the guests had finished breakfast and were now in the entryway, dressed in swim trunks and cover ups and sun hats, on their way to the beach. "You're a suspect."

The words felt silly coming out of my mouth. I had to be wrong. There was no way Shep suspected Page of anything. But I also knew they were true. Shep's formal behavior and stopping by the house first thing in the morning? It didn't make sense otherwise. He'd moved away from Matthew, but somehow, he'd stumbled into another absurd theory.

"No, I'm not. That's ridiculous," Page said, laughing. But when she looked up at Shep, she seemed to notice for the first time that he wasn't smiling back. "Isn't it?"

Shep shook his head slowly. "We have reason to believe that you may be involved—"

"You've got to be kidding me," Blaire shouted, running down the rest of the stairs, her pink plaid pajama pants making her look younger than she was.

I grabbed her as she ran for the door, afraid she may lunge at Shep. She hated him enough for suspecting her boyfriend, so I could only imagine how much she despised him now that he suspected her mom.

Just then Jude walked into the room, drawn by the commotion, and I saw Page's eyes flit to him and then refocus on Blaire.

"This will all be sorted, honey. Don't worry. I'll be back in a bit," she said.

Remembering the promise I'd made to Page after we first visited Shep to tell him everything we knew about the dead man, never suspecting I'd actually have to follow through with it, I caught her eye and winked. "I'll help. I'll solve it."

Page gave me a soft smile, and then, with an audience composed of her sister, her daughter, her romantic interest, and her bed and breakfast guests, Page held her chin high, walked briskly across the porch and down the stairs, and ducked into the backseat of Shep's outdated patrol car.

CHAPTER 12

Mason assured me for the hundredth time that he had everything handled at the bed and breakfast.

"I've answered phones and made beds before," he said, squeezing my shoulder. "I swear, I can handle this."

"I feel so bad," I said, my head tipping forward. I felt exhausted. Since Page had been driven away in the patrol car that morning, it felt like I hadn't stopped moving. I only ate lunch because Mason shoved a General Store sandwich in my hands and followed me around the house until I'd eaten at least half of it.

"Why? Don't! This is what I'm here for," he said.

I shook my head. "You have the mural to work on. The deadline is coming up soon, right?"

"No," he said, holding a finger in the air, quieting me. "Do not even begin to put my mural on the same level as your sister's freedom. This is more important. Besides, I'm ahead of schedule."

I knew I would never get anywhere with him, I would

never convince him to leave and go back home. And self-ishly, I was glad. I needed Mason there. Blaire was trying to help, but her anger was threatening to shatter into a million pieces at any moment. I needed balance, stability, and Mason provided that.

"Do you know where you're going to start?" Mason asked.

Trying to pick up the case when it was already moving full speed ahead was tough. I had to go back to the beginning and play catch up, following up on the leads Shep had already explored, try to find anything he could have missed.

"I think so," I said, shrugging, "but the problem is that I still don't know why Shep thinks Page may have been involved, aside from the fact that she argued with the man earlier that day. So, I may be following up on something that isn't even pertinent to the case."

Mason pulled me into a quick hug and kissed my fore-head reassuringly. "You'll figure it out."

I smiled up at him, the corner of my mouth feeling heavier than normal. "I sure hope so."

Matthew was back working the front desk of the Marina, and he straightened up as I walked in, hiding his phone under the desk.

"Don't hide your phone on my account," I said.

His narrow face turned upwards in an awkward smile. "Sorry. My parents are cracking down pretty hard since my brush with the law. Blaire isn't here, by the way."

"I know," I said. "I'm actually here to talk about your 'brush with the law.'"

His face fell. "I don't know what you heard, but it wasn't a big deal. I didn't do what Shep—"

I held up a hand to silence him. "I'm not here to bust you or lecture you. Page is in trouble, and I just need to know if you have the dead guy's wallet."

"No," Matthew said before I'd even finished the question. "I told Shep the same thing. It's the truth. I've never stolen anything from a person's body. I simply abide by the schoolyard rule of Finders Keepers. Everything I had was only what I've found lying on the ground."

"That's still stealing," I said.

"And believe me," Matthew said, ignoring me, "there is no shortage of thieves on the island. The amount of people who come around looking for purses and wallets and backpacks they 'lost' on the ferry is astounding. But wait, what is going on with Page?"

"Have you not talked with Blaire?" I asked. After the way Blaire had cried the night before, I assumed she'd have called Matthew the moment he was released by the police. Though, her mother being arrested may have slightly rearranged her priorities.

"Not since yesterday," he said, checking his phone and then setting it face down on the desk.

I quickly filled him in on the situation, his face growing redder every second.

"That idiot wouldn't know how to solve a case if his life depended on it. There is a murderer on the loose, but he had me in his office half the night because of a few lost wallets."

"Did he reveal any details about the case? Do you know anything that isn't public knowledge?" I asked.

Matthew shook his head. "Sorry, I did all of the talking. Shep's interrogation techniques involved asking me the same question over and over. *Did you steal the wallet?* It wasn't exactly sophisticated. He didn't reveal anything."

Crap. I hadn't wanted to admit it to myself, but Matthew was my only lead. I'd been depending on him to point me towards the next clue. Without him, I was back to square one, and I couldn't afford that. Page was in trouble.

"Thanks anyway," I sighed.

Matthew gave me an apologetic smile and I turned to leave. As I did, though, I saw an elderly couple pass by the window. Mr. and Mrs. Smith. I wasn't exactly in the mood to make small talk, so I hung back, hoping they'd keep walking and not see me. Instead, they stopped just beyond the large picture window and hunched together, their heads nearly touching. Unable to keep my curiosity in check, I took a few steps nearer the window and peered around the frame. Mrs. Smith was digging in her small, but bulging purse. I almost assumed Mr. Smith was merely helping his wife find something in her purse and turned away, but then she removed a roll of cash.

A big roll.

I gasped and covered my mouth, even though there was no way the couple could have heard me through the wall.

Mrs. Smith began flipped through the money. From where I stood, I could see that it was mostly small bills—fives and tens—but there were a lot of them. More than any normal person would carry around in their bag. Page and I had both noticed how liberal Mr. Smith was with tipping. He'd tossed Blaire ten dollars just for bringing him a napkin. But we'd chalked it up to him being a generous, rich man. However, suddenly my suspicions were piqued.

I turned back to Matthew. "Have you seen that couple before?"

He followed my finger to Mr. and Mrs. Smith, who had finished counting their wad of cash and were now walking across the road in front of the Marina back towards town.

He squinted and then nodded. "Yeah, almost every day for the last week. They've been riding the ferry to the mainland in the morning and then riding it back in the afternoon."

That was unusual, as well. Mr. and Mrs. Smith weren't from Sunrise Island. They'd come here specifically to sun themselves on the beach, according to Mrs. Smith. So why would they leave the island almost every day?

I couldn't be sure why, but it felt important. Although, I was also aware how desperate I was for a clue. Could I be projecting my desire for a new lead onto an innocent elderly couple? Perhaps, but that wasn't a good enough reason not to check them out.

"They're staying at the bed and breakfast, right?" Matthew asked. I was still too deep in my thoughts to respond, but Matthew lifted his eyebrows and bounced on the toes of his feet. "Is that a clue? Did I just help you crack the case?"

"No case cracking just yet," I said. "But let me know if you notice anything suspicious, alright?"

He eagerly agreed, and I left, hoping I could make it back to the bed and breakfast before the Smiths.

~

It was easy enough to get into Mr. and Mrs. Smith's room. I owned the bed and breakfast, after all, and since Page and I were nowhere near being able to afford a maid, we also did all of the cleaning. The guests were used to seeing us in and out of the upstairs rooms during the day, so no one said a thing as I unlocked Mr. and Mrs. Smith's room —The Victorian—and stepped inside.

They'd rented out our best room, and now that I'd seen the massive wad of cash Mrs. Smith considered "pocket money," I knew why. They were loaded.

The room was a deep burgundy with an intricately carved fireplace that had cost a small fortune to restore, and a lush four-poster bed in the center of the far wall. The Smiths had reserved the room for two weeks, so they'd gone to the trouble of unpacking their suitcases into the mahogany dresser and matching boudoir, and stored their luggage on the top shelf of the closet. On any normal day, I would have appreciated their tidily kept room. On this day, however, it would have been nice if they'd made more of a mess. Then, if I was caught snooping through their drawers, I could argue that I was tidying up.

First, I stripped the bed and replaced the sheets, because as much as I wanted to immediately rummage through their drawers in search of something—I wasn't yet sure what that *something* was—I actually did need to take care of their room. Page and I had watched videos online about how to make a bed to five-star hotel standards, and it required a lot of pulling and tucking that always left me a little breathless. However, it was also a little therapeutic.

When I finished, the new bedding straightened and smoothed to perfection, the dirty linens on a pile in front of the door, I turned to the drawers. I knew it was wrong. Looking through drawers, especially through the drawers of paying guests, was really bad, and Page would almost certainly advise me not to do it. But Page wasn't there to advise me about anything because she had been in an interrogation room for the entire morning and most of the afternoon. Something told me that, perhaps, this instance was an exception.

I started with the bottom drawer because I wasn't yet ready to investigate the undergarments of an elderly couple, and I'd watched a documentary that followed around rehabilitated burglars, and they said they always started with the bottom drawer. It meant they could move on to ransacking the drawer above without having to close the one before it. Apparently, it saved time.

All I found was a mess of Hawaiian t-shirts, tan shorts, and elastic-waisted jeans. The next drawer didn't yield anything more interesting—tall white socks, a pair of black dress pants, and a worn pair of suspenders. I closed the drawer, even though I knew burglars everywhere would disapprove, and prepared myself for the top drawer. Old man underwear were something I hoped to never see until I was married to an old man, but desperate times called for desperate measures. I reached for the drawer and yanked it open, hard and fast, before I could back out.

I jumped back as though a small army of spiders had crawled out of the drawer, though that might have been less worrying than what I'd actually found.

A drawer full of purses, fanny packs, and money clips that put the stash I'd found in Matthew's back seat to shame. One billfold was black with plastic silver spikes, another was covered in pink stones, yet another had the logo of the Houston Texans stamped on the side. I hesitated to touch anything, thoughts of fingerprints and crime scenes popping into my head before I realized I was looking at stolen wallets, not a dead body. Still, I reached into the drawer with nervous fingers, as though the wallets had teeth, and pulled one out. It looked expensive—soft leather, a crystal snap—and when I opened it up, a blond-haired, blue-eyed woman named Hannah Geyser smiled up at me. She had a Kansas driver's license and was an organ donor. The wallet didn't have any cash in it, but it was full of debit cards, credit cards, and punch cards for frozen yogurt and coffee shops. When I pulled out the debit card, a small slip of paper came out with it and fluttered to the floor. I bent to pick it up, and immediately recognized it as a ticket to the Houston Museum of Fine Arts. It was time stamped for three days ago.

It was stolen. There was almost no other explanation. Unless, of course, a 20-something girl from Kansas who was visiting Texas on vacation decided to willingly hand over her wallet to an elderly couple. Though, that seemed rather far-fetched.

Mr. and Mrs. Smith weren't rich—at least not by conventional means. They were thieves. They rode the ferry morning and evening, stealing from other passengers on the boat and, most likely, from people on the mainland. Even as the thought formed in my mind, I couldn't wrap my head around it. Mr. and Mrs. Smith were so nice. She reminded me of my own grandmother. Though, that was why they had so many purses and wallets. No one would suspect a sweet elderly couple of robbing them. They used their age to their advantage. In a way, I was almost impressed.

Almost.

I quickly dug through the drawer, opening every wallet and purse, unzipping every zipper, and unclasping every clasp, to check IDs. The Smiths had stolen from people all over the country, though the majority were from Texas, and based on the driver's license photos, they did not discriminate. They had IDs from every age and race and sex. Apparently, no one was immune to trusting the elderly. However, there was no sign of the dead man's ID in here. I studied every picture until my eyes felt watery and raw, but he wasn't there. Though Mr. and Mrs. Smith were definitely thieves, and I was going to have to keep a serious eye on their luggage at check out to ensure they didn't rob us blind, they hadn't stolen the dead man's wallet.

The large clock downstairs chimed, and I realized how much time I'd spent in their room. Far more than was required for a simple linen change. I pulled the top drawer open all the way and used both arms to slide the purses and billfolds on top of the dresser into the open drawer, and then pushed it closed. I scooped up the dirty sheets piled in front of the door and hurried out of the room and into the hallway.

No sooner had the Smiths' door closed behind me than I heard footsteps on the stairs. I said a silent prayer of gratitude that I hadn't been caught snooping through an elderly man's drawers, dumped the sheets down the laundry chute hidden behind a cabinet door in the hallway, and turned to face whoever was coming up the stairs.

I'd assumed it was the Smiths or Page or one of the other guests, but instead, it was Sheriff Shep. He had on his tan uniform, though it looked creased with wear and a bit dingier than usual, and he had a fine layer of stubble across his entire face to go along with his thick mustache. He looked exhausted.

Behind him, small and nervous, was Page.

I moved towards them, eyes narrowed. I wanted to hit Shep. Police officer or not, he deserved it for holding my sister at the police station all day. "What's going on?"

Page jumped ahead of Shep and grabbed me by the shoulders, already trying to calm me down. "It's fine. I'm fine. Shep just wants to take a look around," she said.

"Do you have a warrant?" I asked, leaning around Page to block Shep's view of the hallway.

"I let him in," Page said. "We have nothing to hide."

"So? You should still make him get a warrant. I bet he couldn't get one because they don't have enough evidence on you. No judge in their right mind would issue a warrant because of suspicion," I said.

Shep didn't seem to have the energy to spar with me. Instead, he kept his eyes straight ahead and moved down the hallway. When he came to Page's bedroom door, he stopped. "This one?"

Page nodded, and Shep stepped inside.

"What are you doing?" I hissed.

"I'm clearing my name," Page said. "They think I've done something wrong, and I know I haven't, so I'm going to let them investigate until they're satisfied."

"Do they have something on you?" I asked. "You were at the station for a long time. What did he say?"

Page sighed, and I noticed the dark circles under her eyes, the sag in her shoulders. "Shep originally thought Theodore—his name was Theodore, by the way—could have been killed because of money. His bank account was entirely empty and his wallet had been stolen, but when he got in touch with his ex-wife, Margaret, she admitted that she cleared his bank account."

"So, why aren't they investigating her?" I asked, nearly screaming. "Most murders are committed by someone the victim knew. Family members should always be the first suspects."

"She had an alibi," Page said, interrupting my rant. "She claimed that she only emptied the money from his account to ruin his vacation. It was a joint account, and he had been spending it like crazy since they separated. She didn't spend it, though, and she has been living with her parents in Nebraska. She wasn't even in the state on the day he was murdered."

I groaned. "So, his next thought was that you must have killed him?"

Page's eyes were laser focused on me. "I kicked him out of our bed and breakfast and he threatened our business. That's motive."

"Barely!" I said. "People don't kill people over threats that small. Plus, it is *our* business. How does Shep know I didn't kill him?"

"Shh!" Page said, grabbing my shoulders and shaking me. "This isn't a joke, Piper."

"I know it isn't. I'm mad. Shep has no evidence, yet he is treating you like a criminal. This is absurd."

I turned away from Page and took off down the hallway towards her bedroom. How did Page not see how ridiculous this all was? She was acting as if there was any kind of credence to Shep's accusations, which there absolutely was not. It didn't matter that she didn't see it, though. I did, and it didn't matter that Page allowed Shep inside. It was my house, too, and he was going to need a warrant to search anything. I threw the door open.

Shep was on the far side of Page's bed, rising up as if he'd just been searching underneath it. He jumped when the door bounced off the wall, and something dropped to the floor.

"You need to get out, Shep. Come back when you have a warrant," I said.

Page was close behind me. "No, Shep. It's fine. Finish up."

Shep bent down to pick up whatever he'd dropped, not responding or reacting to either of us. Whatever it was had hit the floor and skidded under the bed. He pressed his face against the purple comforter and swung his arm across the floor, blindly searching. Finally, he grabbed it and hauled it up, lifting it into the air.

It was a wallet. Nothing extraordinary about it in any way—worn brown leather, a few rips and snags in the stitching around the edges, and a blue ink stain as big as my pinky nail on one of the corners. There was nothing particularly noteworthy or unusual about the wallet, except that it had clearly belonged to a man, and it clearly did not belong in Page's room.

Shep held it up as though it were the skull in a high school production of *Hamlet*. I just knew he was imagining dramatic theme music playing in the background, adding another layer to the tension.

"What is it?" Page asked, though we all knew that what she'd really meant to ask was, *Whose is it?*

"I think you may already know," Shep said, eyeing us both with a mixture of sadness and suspicion.

"Is it…his?" Page asked.

"We don't know whose it is," I said, doing my best to talk over Page, to cover her words which could potentially be twisted into an admission of guilt. "Why don't you tell us?"

I'd lied. We all knew who the wallet belonged to, and Shep knew we knew, but he still flipped open the old leather and held out the ID towards us as if it were a badge.

Theodore A. Wallace.

CHAPTER 13

"Would you care to explain how his wallet found its way under your bed, Ms. Lane?" Shep asked. Only moments before he'd looked work weary and exhausted, but now his eyes were wide and alert, staring at Page.

Page, on the other hand, looked shell shocked. Her eyes were glassy and unseeing, her mouth hanging open as if she were half asleep.

"Someone put it there," I said.

I knew the explanation was thin and unprovable, but it was the only thing that made sense. Page couldn't have hurt the man, let alone killed him. And up until that very day, she hadn't even known his name. It didn't make sense. Nothing made any sense.

"I'm speaking to the other Ms. Lane," Shep said, giving me a warning look.

We both turned to Page, who looked no more ready to speak than she had the first time he'd addressed her. I turned to her, grabbing her by the upper arms.

"Page," I said, as gently as I could. "You have to help me out here. Explain this."

Page's eyes searched and then locked in on mine, and she shook her head slowly. Her mouth opened and closed several times, the words lodged in her throat, and then she finally croaked, "I don't know."

Shep pulled a plastic bag out of his back pocket and dropped the wallet into it, and I found myself surprised that he even carried around evidence bags. "I'm going to have to ask you to come back down to the station with me," Shep said.

"She doesn't have anything left to tell you," I said, moving to stand in front of Page, who seemed to have entered a catatonic state.

"This is evidence," Shep said. "I can't ignore it."

"Evidence of what? Evidence that the man was at our bed and breakfast before he died? We already told you that! It doesn't prove that Page had anything to do with it," I challenged.

"It was in her bedroom, Piper."

"You busted her daughter's boyfriend for stealing wallets. Ever think maybe he could have left it here? And let's not forget the elderly Bonnie and Clyde sleeping in the room across the hall. They could have stashed it under her bed when they discovered he'd turned up dead."

"Elderly Bonnie and Clyde? What are you talking about?" Shep asked.

I didn't have the energy to explain what I'd found in Mr. and Mrs. Smith's room. I needed Shep out of my house. I needed to talk to Page. I needed a minute to stop and think about what was happening around me, so I could piece it together.

"Leave," I said, my voice steady and even, despite the adrenaline-fueled shake that had set into my arms and legs. "Either arrest her or get out. She doesn't have to go anywhere with you."

Shep hesitated, staring at me. He knew I was right, but he was trying to figure out a way around it. Finally, he closed the zipper of the plastic evidence bag containing the wallet and stomped past us, leaving behind the musty scent of sweat and sun block.

Mason, Blaire, and Jude were sitting at the dining room table, each of them staring down at their own folded hands, saying nothing. When Page and I walked into the room, they all jumped to their feet.

"What happened?" Mason and Blaire asked at the same time.

Jude looked from Page to me and then back to Page, eyes widening as he took in her pale, listless state. "Did he find anything?"

"Of course he didn't find anything," Blaire said. "Mom is innocent."

I pursed my lips and lowered Page into one of the wooden chairs. She sunk into it gratefully and lowered her face into her hands.

"Right?" Blaire asked, suddenly not sure. She took the chair next to her mom, placing her hand gently on her shoulder. "He didn't find anything, did he?"

Blaire's fear seemed to wake Page up. She placed her

hand over Blaire's and patted it in the soft way only moms know how to do. "He found the man's wallet."

"The dead guy's wallet?" Blaire asked, leaning back as though the sentence was a bomb and she didn't want to be hit by the shrapnel.

"Theodore's," Page said, nodding her head.

Mason looked at me, his eyes asking a question I couldn't answer. It didn't make sense. Everyone, whether they admitted it or not, was looking at me to solve this. They expected me to have all of the answers like I had in the past, but I didn't have a single clue. And it was terrifying. Sure, Mr. and Mrs. Smith had a drawer full of purses and wallets, but that only proved that they were thieves. It didn't mean they were murderers. They could have planted the wallet in Page's room, but something about that felt wrong. Why would they plant the wallet so close to where they kept their own stash? Surely, they would have wanted to get it as far away from themselves as possible.

"Why did they suspect you in the first place?" Jude asked, taking an almost imperceptible step away from Page, leaning against the dining room door as if he had half a mind to sprint out the door.

"Witnesses saw me arguing with him in front of the bed and breakfast," she said.

"And that's all they said?" Jude asked. "They didn't see you near the crime scene or anything like that?"

Jude's line of questioning suddenly felt less curious and more suspicious. Sure, he didn't know Page well, but I wasn't going to stand by and let him accuse her of something she didn't do. Not in my house. I shot him a dark look, and he shrank back ever so slightly.

Page didn't seem to take any offense from his question and simply shook her head. "They had almost nothing on me, so I agreed to let Shep search my room to put the whole thing to rest, and now he has the wallet. I have no idea how it even got there."

"Maybe he left it here when he tried to check in and it just found its way up to your room?" Blaire suggested, her tone prodding, as if she wanted to lead her mother to the explanation. As if the answer were locked away in Page's mind, and all she needed to do was fiddle with the padlock before it would snap open and we'd have all of the answers.

Page's shoulders lifted slightly, and then sunk down even further than before. "I don't know. Maybe. I don't remember, but…maybe."

For as long as I could remember, Page had always had all the answers. She faced down every challenge that came her way without complaint, but now I could see weariness creeping in. Since we'd discovered the identity of the dead man, Page had been lost, worried. I'd never seen her so flustered before. If she wasn't my sister, I may have even suspected her. But she was my sister, and I knew it was impossible.

"Why don't we let Page get some rest," I said, more of a command than a suggestion. "It has been a very long day and we all need to process."

Jude rushed off, not eager to insert himself any more than he already had into our family drama, and Mason offered to stay and help take care of things.

"No, really, you've done enough," I said.

"Are you sure?" He grabbed my hand. "I don't mind."

"You have work to do, I'm sure, and you've already spent so much time here. I'll call if we need anything."

"You promise?"

I smiled and squeezed his fingers. "I swear."

Blaire stayed seated at the table. "Why don't you get out of the house for a bit," I suggested. "You need some normalcy in your life. Why don't you call Matthew?"

She tensed. "He's at work."

"That's never stopped you before," I said.

"Yeah, Blaire. I'm fine. Go have fun," Page said.

"I don't want to," Blaire snapped. Just as quickly, her face softened into an apology. "I'm just going to go to my room."

When her footsteps were halfway up the stairs, Page sighed. "She shouldn't have to be dealing with this. It's my mess, not hers."

"This isn't your mess. None of us should be dealing with it," I said. "But we'll sort it all out, and you'll be off the hook soon."

"I hope you're right," Page said, her head shaking almost imperceptibly. She looked defeated, which scared me. Despite her innocence, Page really thought she might take the rap for this.

I followed Page all the way up the stairs and into her room.

"You don't have to help me," she said, giving me a smile that I didn't believe.

"I'm just assisting my elders," I joked.

"I'm not an elder!"

"You're seven years older than me. That makes you my elder," I said.

She rolled her eyes at me, but let me pull back her comforter and help her lay down.

"Do you want anything? Water? A snack?" I asked.

Page shook her head. "I just need to take a nap. Hit reset on my body and this day. Thanks, though."

I was about to leave when Page stopped me. "Actually, could you plug in my phone? It's almost dead."

I took it from her and bent down to plug it into the charger cord laying on the floor. As I did and her phone vibrated to let me know it was charging, I noticed a small piece of paper laying on the floor where Shep had found the wallet earlier. I reached for it, my hand disturbing the dust bunnies that had built up under the bed since we'd moved in a few months before.

The piece of paper was small, ripped from the corner of a lined notebook, and it had seven digits hastily scrawled across it in pencil. It was a phone number.

I stood up, ready to ask Page if she knew whose number it was, but her eyes were closed and her breathing was heavy. Even if she wasn't quite asleep yet, I didn't want to burden her with anything else. Quietly, I tucked the piece of paper into my back pocket and slipped from her room.

By the time I was in the hallway, I'd already pulled the piece of paper from my pocket. I stared at the numbers, willing them to rearrange into a name or a clue. Something.

Could this number have fallen out of Theodore's wallet when Shep dropped it? Could it lead to another suspect? And if it did lead to Theodore's murderer, would Page still be implicated? The number was found under her bed with no proof that it was ever *inside* the wallet. What if the number led to a hit man and then Shep thought Page hired one to kill Theodore? It sounded like the plot of a bad action movie, but I couldn't rule anything out. I'd never be able to forgive myself if I somehow made things worse for Page. I had to investigate this one on my own. Figure out where the number led before I turned it over to the police.

I pulled my phone out of my back pocket and punched the number into my phone, and held it to my ear. It began to ring, and my heart was pounding, not knowing what I'd find at the other end of the line. Then, I realized I was still standing outside of Page's door, and I didn't want her to hear me on the phone and come asking questions, so I ducked into the bathroom across the hallway and shut the door, flipping the lock into place with a dull thud.

The phone rang several more times, and I leaned back against the sink, my foot tapping out a nervous rhythm on the tile floor. Then, finally, a female voice answered.

"Hello."

"Hi," I said eagerly, trying to sound as friendly as possible so the woman wouldn't hang up.

"The number you have reached is not available. Please leave a message at the tone."

Even though I was alone in the bathroom, my face flushed with embarrassment. I'd been fooled by a robotic answering machine voice. When the beep sounded, I had no idea who I was leaving a message for or what I was going to say, so I simply left my phone number and hung up.

Then, before I could change my mind, I pulled my phone back out and pressed Mason's name. It barely rang once before Mason picked up.

"Everything okay?" he asked, slightly breathless.

"Yeah, fine," I said. "I know you just left, but is there any way you could come back?"

I heard a car door shut and the rumble of an engine in the background. He had probably just made it home and gotten out of the car when I called. "Sure, I'm on my way. Did you change your mind about needing help?"

"I just need to run a quick errand and hoped you could keep an eye on things around here while I'm gone."

Within five minutes, Mason was at the bed and breakfast, and within twenty, I was in a rental boat from the Marina. I was going to investigate the crime scene for myself.

CHAPTER 14

The late morning was warm and sticky, but it wasn't a picturesque island afternoon. The sky was a heavy flannel gray, pressing down on me as I made my way across the bay. The motorboat I rented from the Marina was spotted with rust and I had to turn the key a few times before the engine finally turned over, but it was the last one they had left, and so far, it seemed to keep out water. Matthew had apologized for the state of it several times, and I had made a joke about getting the family discount, at which he became incredibly uncomfortable. I had paid the normal amount and left, hoping he wouldn't tell Blaire I'd made him uncomfortable. Blaire would no doubt think I was trying to meddle in her relationship, and I'd have to endure the chill of her icy teenage wrath for at least three days before she forgave me.

I passed jet skiers and college-aged kids on boats much larger than mine as I made my way down the coast towards the cave. They blasted music that sounded tinny and hollow coming across the water, and each of them held a red plastic cup as if they were in a spring break destination spot commercial. When we first moved to the island, that's what I'd imagined life to be like. Maybe not *exactly* like that. I wouldn't be blasting rap music and there would be significantly fewer people on my boat, but I'd pictured going out on the water with Page and Blaire, reading while we suntanned, gossiping about the locals. Now I couldn't picture it. Not after the bodies and the murders. Sunrise Island no longer seemed like the tropical paradise I'd first envisioned. What those kids on the boat didn't know was that it had a dark underbelly. I'd seen it, and I wouldn't be able to forget.

It hadn't taken much asking to uncover where exactly the body was discovered. Though I had done my best to stay out of the investigation, the rest of the island's inhabitants seemed to have done their utmost to be as much a part of it as possible. I'd quietly asked a couple in their mid-fifties if they'd heard about the body, and before I knew it, I was surrounded by six other people. They pointed me in the direction of the cave, but not before telling me all of their theories. I barely listened, except to note that none of them said anything about Page, which was a relief. That news, thankfully, had yet to circulate in the rumor mill. I wondered how long we had before it did.

I motored out into the bay and followed the curving coastline until the cave came into view. It was barely a cave. Even from a distance, the sun was bright enough to illuminate the back wall, and the mouth was maybe twenty-five feet wide. Based on the excitement surrounding the cave at the marina, I'd assumed the area would be crowded with curious onlookers and kids searching for a thrill. However, the small cave seemed to be deserted. In fact, everyone seemed to be actively avoiding the area, instead cramming into the far side of the bay.

I pulled the boat up to a small wooden dock that looked one storm away from falling to pieces, and threw a looped rope around a moss-covered post. The cave was visible just ahead, the opening like a dark mouth opened wide, ready to swallow anyone who came too near. A chill ran down my spine and I had to remind myself that Theodore was no longer there. He was in a morgue somewhere far away, and this was just a normal stretch of beach.

Shep never said whether they thought Theodore had been killed at the cave or killed somewhere else and moved to the cave, but I immediately believed it to be the latter. Perhaps it was purely to protect myself from the thought that I was standing in a place where a man was violently murdered. Either way, the ground didn't look to be disturbed, at least, not any more than normal. There were a lot of footprints moving from the dock to the mouth of the cave, probably from the many police officers and EMTs who had arrived after the body was discovered, but otherwise, everything looked normal. No obvious signs of a struggle or blood stains. Just an empty cave and an empty beach.

I wasn't sure what I'd expected to find. Aside from the phone number I'd already called, I had zero leads and zero suspects, unless I truly believed Mr. and Mrs. Smith were capable of murder, which I didn't. Going to the cave was a last-ditch effort at picking up a trail, and it was disappointing to realize there was nothing there to find. It was starting to make sense why Shep had latched on to Page as a suspect. She had an argument with the victim the day he died, he threatened our business, and now Shep had found the man's wallet under her bed. In the face of so few clues, those three things, while mostly circumstantial, were significant.

I gave the shallow cave one last look over before leaving. The walls had been graffitied, no doubt by local kids, and featured an eclectic assortment of indecipherable tags and hearts with initials inside them. Soda bottles faded from sun and water littered the floor of the cave, but otherwise the ground was clear.

I sighed, and trudged back through the sand towards the boat. In the short amount of time I'd been on the beach, the sun had entirely disappeared behind clouds, and the bay was considerably less busy. I lowered into the boat and flipped the headlight on even though it wasn't quite dark enough to require one, deciding it was better to be cautious. As I did, the boat bobbed with an incoming wave, and the headlight caught on something in the sand just in front of the boat.

Not quite ready to give up and desperate for any clue, I scrambled back out of the boat and sunk to my knees on the beach, sifting through the sand. I had a flashback to the day many months back when I'd done the same thing, only I was uncovering a human body. I pushed the thought from my mind and sifted through the sand until my fingers caught something large and metal. I pulled it from the sand.

It was a mermaid. A metal one. Seashells hung in her hair, and her arm was raised in a wave. More seashells covered her breasts, and her tail was bent upward, the curve of it resting on a flat piece of metal. It looked like it was meant to screw onto the front of something like a car emblem. I rotated her and noticed deep scratches marred the side of her tail. I crawled forward towards the dock and found a gouge in the wood at the same height as the bow of my boat. At some point, someone had pulled in a little too close to the dock and lost the mermaid. Could it have been from the murderer's boat? Sure, but it also could have been any of hundreds, if not thousands, of other boats. The mermaid had been almost completely covered in sand, which didn't lend credence to the idea that it was a relatively new inhabitant of the island. It could have been buried in the sand for months before I arrived. Though, it did have a rather nice sheen to it.

I couldn't make up my mind, so I decided to call Shep.

"Hello," he said, clearly not thrilled to be receiving a call from me. "If you're calling to yell at me, I'd prefer if you didn't. I'm only doing my job."

"I found something," I said. "On the beach in front of the cave."

"*The* cave?" he asked.

"Yeah. I came out here to—"

"I thought you weren't going to get involved," he said. I could hear the smugness in his voice. The silent "I told you so" between the words.

"That was before you tried to pin the crime on my sister," I said.

There was a beat, and then Shep sighed. "Unfortunately, it would be wrong of me to accept your help now. Your sister is our main suspect. I couldn't trust your judgment."

"I'm not calling to give you theories. I'm calling to present a hard piece of evidence. It's a mermaid."

Shep laughed, and it sounded as if he choked on his coffee.

"A metal mermaid. Like a hood ornament, but for a boat."

"Okay?"

I could tell he wasn't taking me seriously, and I wanted to yell, though he'd expressly asked me not to. I took a deep breath. "I found it in the sand near the dock. It looks like somebody pulled a boat up here, scratched the dock, and knocked it off. It could be a clue."

Shep didn't say anything for a few seconds.

"Shep?"

"Yeah, yeah, I'm here. Listen," he said. "I wrote everything down. We are looking over the security footage from the Marina. If the mermaid becomes important, I'll be sure to let you know."

Shep didn't want to come down to the cave and look. He didn't even want me to bring the mermaid to him. Was he right about me? Was my judgment off because Page was involved? Had I just found a piece of trash on the beach and tried to report it to the police? I'd always tried to trust my instincts, but now I wasn't so certain I could. Everything in me was telling me to do anything and everything I could to clear Page's name of this murder, and that desire was clouding my thoughts. I couldn't look at anything objectively anymore.

Frustrated, I pushed the mermaid into my pocket, the base of it sticking out, and climbed back into the boat. A storm seemed to be approaching, and I didn't want to be out on rough waters in such a small boat. I pulled in the rope, started the engine, and took off towards the Marina, the motor shattering the dark glass of the bay, churning it into bubbles and waves.

I must have spent longer at the cave than I'd thought because the vacationers and boaters I'd seen before had mostly cleared out by the time I pulled the boat up to the dock. As I passed every boat, I studied the bows, looking for a scrape, a sign that this mermaid was missing from her perch. I saw nothing.

When I got to the front office, the lights inside were dim, and a note had been stuck to the front door.

"Closed for lunch. Place keys in drop box."

An arrow had been drawn in thick sharpie and was pointing down to the mail slot. How professional. Still, with no other choice, I dropped the rental boat's key through the mail box, heard it clatter on the tile floor inside, and left.

When I got back Blaire was in the sitting room with her feet up on the coffee table—Page would have kicked her feet off the coffee table in an instant—and a book held in front of her face. She didn't look up when I walked in, and for a moment, everything felt normal. Shep had never suspected Page of the murder and this was any normal day in our lives. Then, Blaire met my eyes. Hers were red-rimmed and swollen with tears.

"Oh, Blaire," I said, sounding remarkably like my own mother. *Bless your heart, Piper.* "What's wrong?"

I knew what was wrong. Everything. Her boyfriend and her mother had both been suspected of murder. And even if they hadn't been, she'd been moved away from her school and her friends to an island where three people had been murdered in as many months. If that didn't give her a good excuse to sit around and cry, I didn't know what would.

"Nothing," she said. "I'm just reading."

Clearly, she didn't want to talk, and I didn't want to push her. I tried to pretend it wasn't obvious she'd been crying.

"Where's your mom?"

"In her room," she said. Her voice was thick with unshed tears. "Jude has been up there with her for a while."

She offered up the information freely and casually, but I had to wonder whether that wasn't why she'd been crying. Her parents had been divorced for almost a year now, but that probably didn't make seeing her mom with another man any easier. Blaire had been given the option to live with her dad, but she'd chosen to stay with her mom, even though it meant moving away to Sunrise Island. He'd cheated on Page, and Blaire couldn't forgive him so easily. However, did she see Page and Jude's relationship as cheating? Had she expected her mom and dad to make up eventually?

"I'm sure they're just talking," I said.

Blaire raised an eyebrow at me, but didn't say anything. I could tell she didn't believe me, and I wasn't sure if I believed me, either. Page had only begun to dip her toes in the world of dating, but she seemed pretty smitten with Jude.

Just then, Mason came into the room.

"I thought I heard you come in. Did you find anything?" he asked, a laundry basket of towels balanced on his hip. He looked like a stay-at-home mom from a fifties sitcom.

"What does he mean *find anything*?" Blaire looked from me to Mason and back again. "Where were you?"

"Nowhere." The word came out too quickly. Much too quickly to be believable, but Blaire hadn't answered me about why she was crying, so I didn't feel too bad evading her question. Besides, I didn't want to get Blaire's hopes up. I hadn't found anything useful on the stretch of beach —save for a metal mermaid, which might actually just be a piece of trash—so I decided in that moment it would be best to keep the whole operation under wraps. I'd only come forward with information when I had something concrete and useful.

Blaire rolled her eyes and closed her book with a snap, mumbling as she left the room. "I'm not a little kid."

"No one said you were a little kid," I called after her. Things were always so hard with Blaire. I never knew where I should fall on the spectrum of friend to authority figure. "Where are you going?"

"My room," she said, stopping on the stairs to give me a 'duh' look.

"I saw that Matthew closed the Marina early. Why don't you go hang out with him?"

I was definitely no professional when it came to doling out advice, but telling a distressed person to go hang out with friends and get some fresh air was textbook.

Her face went pale and I saw a brief flash of pain in her eyes before she returned to her surly teenager routine. "I'll be in my room."

"She's pleasant," Mason joked when Blaire slammed her door shut.

I laughed, trying to brush it off, but something about her reaction struck me as more than teen angst.

"So," Mason said, turning to me, his voice low and conspiratorial. "What did you find?"

I took the mermaid out of my pocket and explained it and the gouges on the dock. Unlike Shep, Mason seemed excited by the news.

"That's a huge lead!" he said.

I shrugged and pursed my lips. "Maybe."

"Maybe? How many boats have mermaid ornaments? Not many, I'd bet. Those old men down at the Marina know every boat down there inside and out. It wouldn't take much asking to find out who it belonged to," he said.

Mason was talking fast, his voice rising as he got more and more excited, and I was feeling flustered. I'd avoided telling Blaire about the mermaid because I hadn't wanted to get her hopes up but, in a way, I'd also wanted to protect myself. Solving the last two murder cases had been a fluke more than anything else. There had been a whole lot of luck and very little skill involved. And now, Page was counting on me. Blaire was counting on me. My family's existence rode on me solving this case, and I wasn't certain I could do it.

"It was partially buried in the sand," I said, trying to temper Mason's enthusiasm. "It could have been there for months or years for all we know."

Mason turned the mermaid over in his hands and shook his head. "No, this looks new. Recently polished. We'd notice a lot more tarnish if it had been lying in the sand for months."

I knew he was right, but I still didn't want to allow myself to fully believe it. I decided to change the subject. "What we really need to focus on is how the wallet got into the bed and breakfast. That is the only physical tie between Page and Theodore. If we can sever that, Shep doesn't have a case."

"You still don't think it could have been Mr. and Mrs. Smith?" Mason asked.

I'd briefly filled him in on the purses and wallets I'd found in Mr. Smith's top drawer before I'd left for the Marina, and he confirmed what a great cover the elderly couple had. I'd had to assure him *three* times that I was, in fact, not joking, and he still wasn't sure he believed me.

I shook my head. "It doesn't make any sense. You don't steal that many wallets by being an idiot, and it would be idiotic for them to throw Theodore's wallet across the hall. They could have wiped it and dumped it in the ocean or buried it in the sand near where the body was found. Heck, they could have dumped it in the bottom of any random dumpster on the island and it likely never would have been seen again."

"So, what's our theory?" Mason asked.

Although it was nice to have someone to bounce ideas off of, I could feel the weight of Mason's expectations, as well. He expected me to know what came next, to have a lead to follow, and I didn't.

"Well," I said, pausing to try and give myself time to come up with something more clever to say than '*Page didn't do it.*'

"Somebody must have planted the wallet under her bed," I finally said, looking at him out of the corner of my eye, hoping he wasn't disappointed.

He nodded. "Okay. So, it had to be someone who had access to the house."

"That narrows down the list," I said, getting excited. I hadn't expected my theory to lead to anything more than an awkward silence, but Mason was right. Whoever dropped off the wallet couldn't have just thrown it through an open window. It was placed under Page's bed, which meant someone had to have been *inside* the house to plant it.

"And it seems important that the wallet was inside Page's room."

I nodded again, my brain working overtime. He was right. I hadn't really considered it, but if someone had simply wanted to ditch the wallet, they could have left it anywhere—in a bush, on the porch. Why would someone risk sneaking into Page's room to hide it there?

A lightbulb went off in the back of my mind. "They framed her. Someone wanted to frame her."

"You think someone specifically targeted her?" he asked.

"Think about it. Shep said that there were witnesses to her fight with Theodore that day. Whoever killed him must have known that he'd argued with Page earlier in the day, making her a likely suspect. Somebody used that fight to frame her. It's the only thing that makes sense."

"Okay, so who knew about the fight and had access to the bed and breakfast?" he asked.

My hopes, which were soaring moments ago, come crashing down to the ground in a fiery heap. "Every single guest who was checked in," I said, defeated.

Then, two puzzle pieces clicked together in the back of my mind, and I reached out and grabbed Mason's forearm, my fingers squeezing while I thought. Blaire's bad attitude, Matthew's weirdness back at the Marina. Who was the only person, aside from Mr. and Mrs. Smith, with access to the bed and breakfast and a penchant for stealing?

A smile broke across my face. Perhaps I did have a knack for solving these cases.

"I need to call Shep."

CHAPTER 15

My initial excitement over having a new lead turned to dread as the phone rang. Matthew was Blaire's boyfriend. Her first boyfriend, as far as I knew. The night he was in the interrogation room, she'd spent the whole evening crying for him. I didn't want to be the person who caused her pain. However, I also couldn't let a murderer walk free.

My theory was still pretty thin, but it made sense. It made sense even when I really didn't want it to. Even when I searched for any crack or flaw in the idea. At first, I thought perhaps my desperation to save Page was clouding my judgment. I wanted her name cleared so badly that I would implicate almost anyone. Mason assured me, however, that I wasn't being biased. Matthew truly seemed like he could be the guy.

Not only did Matthew have access to the house—including the second floor, because I'd caught him scaling the trellis under Blaire's window on more than one occasion—but Blaire would have certainly told him about the fight Page and Theodore had. That argument, no matter how small it may seem to the average person, was more excitement than we'd seen around the bed and breakfast since Nathaniel Sharp's body had turned up on the beach, and Blaire wouldn't have been able to keep it to herself for long. Plus, as much as Matthew had tried to minimize his actions, he'd stolen from people. I'd seen a stash of wallets in his grungy backseat for myself.

The next portion of the theory, though, was even hard for me to swallow. Making the leap from wallet thief to murderer was extreme, and I couldn't quite imagine the quiet, lanky boy who'd sold me a bike my first week on the island as a murderer. That was the one piece that didn't quite fit.

After several long rings, Shep finally picked up the phone. After everything that had happened the last few days, I wouldn't have been surprised if he'd decided to ignore me.

"Piper," he said, his voice a warning I did not intend to heed.

"Shep." Two could play at that game.

He sighed, his exhale making the phone go staticky for a few seconds. "What's up?"

"You have to talk to Matthew Pelkey again," I said.

There was a long pause. "*You* want *me* to talk to Matthew Pelkey?"

"Yes."

He let out a bark of laughter that made me jump. "You're joking, right? You have to be joking."

"I think Matthew may have—"

"This is so rich," Shep said, talking over me. "The other day I was the biggest buffoon on the face of the earth for suspecting a young kid, and now that I've moved on, you want to tell me you agree?"

I knew it looked bad. I'd insisted I wanted nothing to do with the investigation and then belittled Shep's detective work. Now that my sister was in trouble, though, I was suddenly agreeing with Shep and tracking down leads. I'd be suspicious if I were him, too, but that didn't change the fact that I had changed my mind about Matthew.

"I know I asked for your help, Piper," Shep continued, "but that doesn't mean I'm not capable of conducting my own investigation and that doesn't mean that I will default to your opinions."

Shep and I disagreed on a few points—mainly his ability to conduct an investigation—but now was not the time to bring that up. In fact, it would never be time to bring that up. I needed Shep's help, and people weren't normally willing to offer you assistance after you told them they were incapable of doing their job.

"I know, Shep," I said, imbuing each word with as much humility as I could muster. "And I was hasty to dismiss your concerns about Matthew early on because he is dating my niece and he is just a young kid, but I've come around to your way of thinking. It makes sense."

There was a long pause. "How so?"

Despite what Shep had said, he was eager to hear my theory, probably to determine whether he'd missed anything important. Part of me wanted to focus on this and do a little "I told you so" dance, but I played it cool.

"First, Theodore was missing his wallet, and Matthew is a confirmed thief. Second, Matthew knew Page and Theodore had been in a fight earlier that day. Third—"

"Wait," Shep said. "Matthew wasn't the one who told me about the argument between your sister and the deceased. He wasn't even a witness to the event."

"He's dating my niece, though, who was a witness," I said.

Shep didn't say anything right away, and I gave him a minute to catch up. Finally, he made a humming noise in the back of his throat.

I continued. "Third, Matthew had access to our house. He is upstairs near the bedrooms often, and it would not have been difficult to slip into Page's room and leave the wallet under her bed. Plus, he also works very near where the body was discovered. It would have been easy for him to take one of the rental boats out to the cave and deposit the body without anyone noticing."

A slight shiver ran down my spine as I wondered whether Matthew had used the same boat he'd rented out to me earlier that afternoon to deposit Theodore's body on the beach. Had he found some kind of perverse pleasure in watching me motor away in the boat he'd used to dispose of a body? Surely not. Suspected murderer or not, I couldn't imagine Matthew being quite that callous.

"Those are compelling points," Shep said.

Finally, I felt like I could see the light at the end of this tunnel. I didn't know what could have made Matthew hurt a man he didn't know—perhaps a burglary gone wrong—but my goal was not to determine motive. It was to save my sister, and I'd done that.

"Unfortunately," Shep said, letting out a long breath. "Matthew has an alibi."

My heart sank. The long tunnel I'd been walking down turned pitch black, not even a tiny pinprick of light visible in the distance. I was standing in darkness and I couldn't even tell which way was up.

"What do you mean?" I asked, hoping that somehow 'alibi' didn't mean what I thought it meant. Hoping that I'd misunderstood Shep.

"He closed the Marina early that day and went out on a date," Shep said, and suddenly I could hear the smugness in his voice. He was relishing this. Relishing the fact that he had more information than I did, that he'd solved a part of the case that I was still hung up on. Shep loved that I had been wrong. He loved it enough that he had let me spill the entire theory to him while he just sat and listened, knowing it was pointless. If I could have reached through the phone and slapped him, I would have.

As my anger ebbed and then flowed, a thought flickered in the back of my mind. As I fanned it, the thought flared to life and suddenly everything was illuminated. "That's wrong," I said. "Matthew wasn't on a date that night. Blaire was home all night. I remember."

Shep sighed. "All I can tell you is that he gave me an alibi and I interviewed the girl and she confirmed it."

The girl? Why was he talking about Blaire like that? He knew her. Why wasn't he using her name?

Then, a sick feeling settled in my stomach. My mouth went slack, and Mason, who had been standing next to me trying to decipher how the conversation was going, was staring at me with confusion on his face.

What's wrong? he mouthed.

"The girl wasn't Blaire?" I asked.

"The girl was not Blaire," Shep said slowly, and this time, there was no smugness in his voice. I could tell he felt sorry, and I was grateful to him for that.

"Thanks, Shep," I said.

"Of course," he said.

We hung up, and I felt nauseous. How was I supposed to tell Blaire that her first boyfriend had cheated on her?

"What happened?" Mason asked, eager to understand why my face was volleying between tense anger and sadness.

I looked at him, my fist clenching at my side. "I'm going to kill Matthew Pelkey."

CHAPTER 16

Blaire's door was opened just a crack. I could see the corner of her bed, her foot with black-polished toes hanging off the end. When I knocked, she stiffened.

"I'm busy."

"I just want to talk to you for a minute," I said, pushing the door open.

She rolled over on her back, her gaze focused on the ceiling. "I'd tell you to go away, but I know you wouldn't listen."

"Got that right, kid," I said, flopping down next to her on the bed.

She smiled slightly, but moved quickly to bite it down. We lay there for a minute, a heavy, expectant silence stretching between us.

"Talk," Blaire commanded, rolling over onto her side so she was propped up on her elbow. "You're freaking me out. Is this about mom?"

I shook my head, and then thought better of it. "Well, a little."

She raised her eyebrows at me, clearly impatient.

I twisted my nervous fingers in her bedspread, a fraying quilt Page and my mom had made for her when she was born. They'd spent months working on it while Page was pregnant, arguing over every square and stitch. But when they finally finished it the week before Blaire was born, they were so pleased with themselves, they forgot all about the fighting.

"I've been working on the murder investigation to try and clear your mom, right?"

Blaire nodded, her eyes wide and nervous. She put up a tough front, but she had the biggest heart of anyone I'd ever known. I hated that I was going to be the one to break it.

"Well, I started working on the theory that someone planted the wallet in your mom's room, which narrowed down the suspect list to anyone who had access to the house." I hesitated, wishing that Blaire could somehow read my mind so I wouldn't have to say the words aloud. "That list included Matthew."

Blaire sighed, her eyes rolling skyward. "Aunt Piper, Matthew didn't—"

"Just hear me out," I interrupted. "A lot of different clues pointed to Matthew, so I called Sheriff Shep, and—"

"Matthew didn't do an—" she said, trying to talk over me.

I was on a roll, and if I didn't spit it out now, I never would. I continued, despite her interruption. "I called Sheriff Shep, and told him my theory, and he said—"

"MATTHEW CHEATED ON ME!" Blaire shouted. As soon as the words left her lips, she rolled onto her stomach, her face buried in her quilt. "He cheated on me," she repeated, her words muffled by the blanket.

I sat there in stunned silence for a moment, watching Blaire's back rise and fall with her heavy breathing. After a few seconds she rolled over, her face peeking up at me, cheeks flushed.

"How did you know?" I asked.

She flopped over onto her back and sighed, shaking her head. "I asked why Shep let him go, and he seemed really guilty, so I began to suspect maybe he did kill the guy. But then he told me the truth."

"He told you?" I asked.

She shrugged. "I guess being a giant jerk is preferable to being a murderer."

I couldn't help myself. I laughed. Blaire shot me a glare.

"Sorry," I mumbled. "Why didn't you tell anyone?"

"Would you have told anyone if Mason cheated on you?" she asked. "I was embarrassed."

She had a good point. I probably would have kept the information a secret for as long as possible. "You shouldn't be embarrassed. He should be. He let an amazing girl go."

Blaire rolled her eyes, but I saw a small smirk paint the edges of her mouth.

"So, who do you think did it if it wasn't Matthew?" she asked, changing the subject. Though her expression didn't change, I could see the tension in the furrow of her brow.

I wished I could tell her I had another strong lead, and

I was hours away from cracking the case, but I couldn't lie. I had a metal mermaid, a phone number that had so far been a bust, and a couple useless theories.

"You could search the phone number," Blaire said when I told her how the case was going.

"What?"

"Type the number in a search engine and see what pops up," she said. "It might give you a name or a business or something like that."

How had I not thought to do that? I reached out, grabbed her by the cheeks, and left a huge kiss on her forehead. "You're a genius."

She grimaced and wiped away the slobber left behind by my kiss. "Remind me never to help you again," she called after me as I ran for the door and sprinted down the hallway.

I grabbed the tablet we kept at the front desk for scheduling and taking payments, and opened the web browser. The phone number was still in my back pocket, and I pulled it out, smoothing it on the desk with both hands. My fingers tapped anxiously on the wood as I waited for the ancient tablet to open a browser. Finally it did, and I typed in the number and hit 'search.'

A list of results popped up, and my shoulders sagged. For some reason I'd expected to type in the number and receive one result—the name of the murderer. Obviously, that was an unrealistic dream, and I would have to do some work. I hunched over the tablet and began flicking through the results, dismissing them one by one.

"How did she take it?"

I jumped, not realizing anyone had come up behind me.

"Sorry." Mason lifted his hands in apology.

I placed a hand over my heart, and shook away my nervous energy. "She already knew," I said.

I explained the entire conversation to Mason, and then told him about the phone number.

"Why didn't you just look it up online?" he asked.

I flopped my arms on the desk. "Apparently, I'm the only one living in the Stone Ages, because I didn't even think of doing that until Blaire mentioned it," I said.

Mason laughed and read the screen over my shoulder. "Found anything yet?"

I shook my head. "Not yet."

I clicked the next link, and it pulled up a sales site. Someone was selling a boat.

2009 Seadoo Challenger 430 HP Power Boat - $12,300

There was a phone number listed for offers and questions, but no name. I held up the piece of paper, and my heart nearly stopped.

"Does it match?" Mason asked.

I nodded my head, still unable to believe it.

A series of pictures were attached to the ad, and I clicked on one, enlarging it. The boat was small, definitely more for watersports than anything else. From the side, it looked like a killer whale—a black curve, like a brush stroke, moved from the back, grew thicker in the middle, and tapered out at the front. It was framed by thick bands of white on the top and bottom. I swiped to the next picture and it was a close-up of the inside—the driver's seat and the benches in the back for passengers. I knew almost nothing about boats, despite living on an island, but this one looked nice—clean and tidy, no rips or stains on the upholstery. I swiped to the next and final picture, and if I'd been holding the tablet, I would have dropped it.

The photographer had taken an artsy picture from the front of the boat. The bow was in sharp focus, while the rest of the boat and the background had gone blurry. Sitting in the center of the photo, perched proudly on the bow, was the metal mermaid.

"No way," Mason breathed next to me.

I pulled out my phone and punched in the phone number again. It rang several times, and this time, I did not allow myself to be fooled by the robotic answering machine. When the phone beeped, I quickly expressed my interest in the boat, left my number again, and hung up.

"Do you think they'll call back?" Mason asked.

I shrugged. "Probably not, but it's worth a shot."

We cycled through the photos too many times to count, searching for anything we could have missed, any clue that could point to who was selling the boat, but we didn't see anything beyond the mermaid.

"Why would Theodore have had this person's number in his wallet?" Mason asked. "Was he on the island to buy a boat or was he the person selling it?"

Mason's question sparked a memory. It flickered in the back of my mind, growing brighter the more I thought on it. "Katie said something to me the day the body was discovered," I said, my voice trailing off while I tried to put the pieces of my fading memory together.

"General Store clerk Katie?" Mason asked.

I nodded and turned to the back wall to try and minimize distractions. My spine pressed against the edge of the desk, but I used the pain to focus my thoughts. "She said that a man came into the store the night before the body was found. He didn't have a wallet, and he asked to use the phone."

"Aside from the missing wallet, I don't see how that is very pertinent," he said, raising an eyebrow.

"She didn't know who he called, but she heard him mention something about needing money to get a boat the next morning," I said, finally opening my eyes and facing Mason. "Katie thought he was talking about catching the morning ferry, but maybe he was talking about buying a boat."

We stared at each other, and I could tell by his downturned eyes and sad smile that Mason was thinking the same thing as me. We didn't have much to go on. My case was a build-it-yourself shelf without the instructions. We knew what it needed to look like, but we were missing some steps. Namely, motive. We could place the boat at the cave and we could loosely connect Theodore to the boat, but we didn't know who wanted to sell the boat or why they would have murdered Theodore. No matter how certain we felt about our lead, we couldn't take it to Shep until we had more proof.

"We can't take this to Shep, but are you going to tell Page?" Mason asked, leaning forward, his elbow on the desk. His dark hair fell over his eye, and I wanted to ditch the case and run away with him. Maybe not forever, but just for a week. Somewhere cold where I could wear a coat and ski. Solving a near endless string of murders makes you crave a vacation.

"Tell Page what?"

Mason looked over my shoulder, and I turned, following his gaze to see Page coming down the stairs. She had foregone her slacks and button downs for a loose pair of black running shorts and a long-sleeve white shirt.

"I thought you were upstairs with Jude?" I asked the question more to gauge her reaction. I wanted to know what exactly they had been doing up there.

Page was no fool. She knew what I was after. "We were talking and he fell asleep," she said, rolling her eyes at me. "But what were you going to tell me?"

"We might have a clue."

Page's eyes went wide, and she took the rest of the stairs two at a time. "What is it?"

I pulled the mermaid out of my pocket and set her on the desk. Page leaned forward so she and the mermaid were eye to eye. "Is this the clue?"

I turned the tablet back on and showed her the boat advertisement. "I found the mermaid on the beach where the body was found, and this boat is currently for sale. Notice the bow."

Page leaned forward, her expression giving away nothing. "And you're certain it's the same boat?"

"Not entirely certain, but it's a pretty good lead, right?" I'd been expecting Page to be excited about the lead, so her hesitation made me unsure. Maybe I was only seeing what I wanted to see.

She nodded. And then with no warning, Page grabbed the mermaid and headed for the front door. "I'll be back," she said.

I grabbed her by the arm. "Where are you going?"

"Tell Jude I went for a walk and I'll be back," she said, her toned arm slipping easily out of my grasp.

I tried to protest, but she was out the door before I could say another word.

CHAPTER 17

"We don't need to worry about your sister, right?" Mason asked for what felt like the hundredth time.

Page had only been gone for fifteen minutes, but we were both on edge, anxious for her to return. It wasn't like Page to leave without saying where she was going, and the way she'd left so suddenly made me think she knew something she wasn't telling me.

"I'm honestly not sure anymore," I admitted. "If you'd asked me that question last week, I would have said that we would never have to worry about Page. But now? I'm not sure."

Sensing how close I was to a complete emotional breakdown, Mason wrapped his strong arm around my shoulders and pulled me into his side. "She'll be fine. I'm sure she will tell us what is on her mind when she gets back."

"I hope so," I said.

Footsteps on the stairs caught my attention and I

turned, expecting to find Blaire. Relief flooded through me when I realized it was Jude. I didn't want to have to try and explain to Blaire where her mom was and what was going on. Blaire insisted she wasn't a little kid, but she had waded through more than her fair share of drama in the last few days, and I didn't want to unnecessarily add more.

"Where's Page?" he asked.

I could see creases from the blankets along his cheek, and his hair was mussed on one side. I'd been doubting whether Page was telling the truth before about him falling asleep, but this confirmed her story.

"We aren't really sure," Mason answered for me.

"She took off fifteen minutes ago," I said.

Jude walked to the desk, his eyebrows pulled together. "Is she okay? Did she get taken back into the station or something?"

I almost smiled, but managed to bite it back. Not because I was glad my sister was gone and potentially a loose cannon, but because Jude so clearly cared about her. She needed that in her life.

"No, nothing like that," I said, calming him. "I showed her some evidence I gathered, and it may have over-whelmed her slightly."

"Oh," Jude bobbed his head, his gaze turned towards the open front door, looking for her. "Poor thing. She has been through a lot the past few days."

Mason and I nodded in agreement.

After a long pause, Jude spoke, his voice barely above a whisper. "What was the evidence? Will it prove she didn't do it?"

I handed him the tablet and explained the phone number and the wallet. Jude nodded as I spoke, his eyes glued to the screen, flipping through the photos of the boat. When I stopped talking, he rose to his feet. "I should go find her."

"She could be anywhere," I said. "Besides, she has been gone almost twenty minutes now. I'm sure she'll be back soon."

He wavered slightly, and I could tell he was trying to make up his mind. Then, he shook his head. "No, I should just go see if I can find her. If not, I'll be back soon."

"Okay, man. Good luck," Mason said. When Jude hustled through the front door, Mason squeezed my shoulders again. "He seems like a good guy."

I agreed. "He seems stable, which is exactly what she needs right now."

~

When the front door opened, I practically lunged for it, yanking it open all the way.

"Oh my," Mrs. Smith said, putting her hand to her heart, eyes wide.

"I am so sorry," I said, smiling to play off how silly I felt. I had been certain Page would be walking through the door any second. A nervous feeling had settled in my stomach since she'd left, and I knew I wouldn't be able to dispel it until I was able to talk with her. "I thought you were my sister."

"Quite alright," Mrs. Smith said. She turned over her shoulder to tell Mr. Smith to hurry up. He was lugging a large canvas bag and I wondered whether they had just finished robbing a bank. I wouldn't put it past them. "And we just saw Page down at the Marina. She seemed very out of sorts."

At that moment, I didn't care whether the couple really had robbed a bank. "How so? Was she alright?"

"Yes," Mrs. Smith said, hauling her purse higher up onto her shoulder. "She was okay, but she seemed pretty flustered. She was down on the docks standing next to that nice young man's boat."

What was Page doing at the docks? She said she was going for a walk. Had she walked all the way to the Marina? That would have taken at least half an hour.

"Which nice young man?" I asked.

"The guest your sister is so smitten with. They are a really darling couple," she said.

"Jude?" I asked.

She nodded. "Yes, that's his name. I do hope everything is okay between the two of them. Page looked quite pale. We offered to give her a ride home, but she insisted she could walk."

I needed to think. I was missing something, and it was obvious.

"Page," Mason said, his voice a warning.

We looked at each other, and all at once the truth came crashing down on me like a tidal wave.

I grabbed the tablet and handed it to Mrs. Smith. "Is this his boat?"

She looked at it, flipping through the photos slowly, her eyes scanning each image at a glacial pace. Finally, after what felt like an eternity, she nodded.

"Yes, this looks like his boat. Only," she pointed to the picture of the mermaid on the front. "His no longer has a mermaid on the front. It must have fallen off. Is he selling the boat?"

"We have to go," I said.

Mrs. Smith continued as if she hadn't heard me. "Mr. Smith and I have been interested in perhaps buying a boat. Of course, at our age, it may be a foolish idea, but we have been considering it."

Mason grabbed his car keys and followed me out the front door. Mrs. Smith mumbled something to Mr. Smith about crazy kids, but I barely heard it. My brain was filtering out everything that didn't matter so I could focus on only the most important thing.

My sister was dating a murderer.

CHAPTER 18

"I'm so stupid. I'm so stupid. I'm so stupid."

"Piper, stop." Mason reached over with his free hand to grab my knee, his eyes focused on the dirt road we were currently tearing down. "This isn't your fault."

"I'm so stupid!" I shouted, pounding my fist into the seat. "I can't believe I didn't see it."

"I didn't, either," he said. "None of us did. This isn't your fault."

"I was just so happy for her. Jude seemed so nice."

Even as the reality of Jude being the murderer washed over me, I couldn't quite believe it. I recalled him smiling shyly at Page while she delivered his breakfast, the way he thanked me for my kindness the first time I met him. He didn't fit my stereotypical image of what a murderer should look like. I wanted to believe I was making a mistake, and clearly Mason did, too.

"So, we're certain Jude did it, right?" he asked, his eyes darting from the road for only a second to glance at me.

I took a deep breath. "Jude showed up at the Bed and Breakfast claiming he wouldn't be able to pay until the next day," I said, glad to be talking it out. "Only, he didn't pay the next day."

"Because he didn't sell the boat," Mason added reluctantly.

"Right," I agreed. "And he didn't sell the boat because Theodore, who was meant to buy the boat, didn't have the money."

"Why exactly didn't Theodore have any money?" Mason asked.

I paused, trying to connect the dots. It felt as if we were reading a book with pages missing, trying to follow the plot line despite large gaps in the story. I sighed, running my hands down my face. "I'm not sure. But when Katie told me about the man who came into the General Store the night Theodore was killed, she said the man spoke on the phone to someone about his bank account. Perhaps he was in some kind of financial trouble."

"Seems strange that he'd show up to buy a boat, then," Mason said. "When I'm tight on cash, I don't typically begin investing in water sports."

"Well it didn't seem like he realized he had financial troubles until he arrived. He was livid when he couldn't pay for his room at the bed and breakfast," I added. Then I remembered. "I think the police told Page something about Theodore's ex-wife having cleaned out his bank account. The ex-wife turned out to be a dead end as a suspect, but at least it explains where the money went."

We sat in silence for a moment, the trees lining the

road whirring by in a wall of green, dust rising up in a cloud behind us.

"None of that explains a motive," Mason said.

He was right. Mrs. Smith positively identified that Jude had the same boat as the one Theodore was likely planning to buy, and the mermaid placed Jude's boat at the location where the body was discovered, but none of that explained what could have driven him to murder.

"Maybe he didn't do it," I said, doubt seeping into my mind. "Maybe there is another explanation."

"Maybe," Mason said hopefully, though I felt the car's speed increase ever so slightly. "The only thing we can do is get to the Marina and make sure Page is okay."

Page. She'd left on foot—no car, no cell phone. We only knew where she was because of Mrs. Smith, but she could have left the Marina by now. She could be anywhere on the island. Wherever she was, I only hoped Jude hadn't found her yet.

Reading my mind, Mason cleared his throat and asked, "Do you think Page recognized Jude's boat in the ad?"

"She had to have recognized it. That's the only thing that explains why she left so quickly," I said.

There was a pause. "Why didn't she say something?" he asked.

This question had been tugging at my thoughts since we left the house. Why wouldn't Page have said that the boat in the ad was Jude's? "I think," I said, the theory still formulating, "she was feeling the way we are now, only one million times worse. She liked Jude, and she didn't want to think he could be capable of murder."

Jude had been her first date since her divorce. He paid

her special attention, made her feel pretty and desired. He gave her the confidence she had lost after sixteen years married to a man who preferred being out on the golf course and working in his shop to spending time with her. Of course she'd want to try and clear his name before mentioning it to anyone. She'd want to be absolutely certain before she ruined any chance they had at a real relationship.

"Let's hope we're all wrong, and he didn't do it," Mason said. "We've been wrong before. This wouldn't be a first."

I nodded. "You're right. There's a chance we're wrong."

The words felt hollow, and rang untrue in my ears. I didn't believe any of it for a second, but if I wanted to hold it together and do my best to protect Page, I had to believe it.

Cars filled the Marina parking lot, and people were crossing the street in front of us, lugging kayaks and inner tubes.

Mason pounded once on the steering wheel. "Do these people honestly have nothing better to do on a weekday afternoon?"

Most of the pedestrians were retired fisherman and young families on the island for a beach vacation, so they didn't have anything better to do, but anxiety was rolling off Mason in waves, so I decided not to say anything. I was too nervous to speak, anyway. From the moment the Marina had come into view, I'd been wordlessly scanning the roads and sidewalks, looking for any sign of Page. Jude had left at least fifteen minutes before us, so he had a good head start. If he was the murderer, he would certainly be after Page. He knew she'd seen the boat and heard our theory. If he was even slightly cunning, which I suspected he was, he would want to silence her before she could spill his secret. And as much as I still wanted to believe Jude liked Page, I had to face the harsh reality, which was that Jude had (most likely) killed before, and he would not hesitate to do it again.

We pulled out of the parking lot and onto the main road only to find it clogged with cars.

"What is with the traffic today?" Mason cried. "This place is a madhouse."

I followed the line of cars and saw a large banner hanging from the Marina.

BOAT SHOW TODAY 12-6

I pointed it out to Mason, and he groaned.

Not a single car was moving, and when Mason shifted into park, my decision was made. I unbuckled my seatbelt and leaned across the console. Mason turned to me, and before he even realized what was happening, I kissed him, thanked him for the ride, and jumped out of the car.

"Be careful," he called.

Despite everything, I smiled to myself. I was dating a man who told me to be careful as I ran down the road to confront a potential murderer. If he wasn't the perfect man for me, then I had no idea who was.

Even through thick clouds, the Texas heat beat down on the asphalt road, and I could feel it radiating through my thin slip-on shoes. A few rowdy men honked at me as I ran along the road, their obnoxiously loud truck horns making me jump, but I did my best to ignore them.

As I neared the Marina, I saw what had caused the back-up. A large truck hauling a boat had jackknifed across the road, blocking traffic in both directions. The driver was halfway hanging out of the driver's side window, his face red and beaded with sweat, while his wife waved her arms frantically to try and direct him out of the tight spot. Nearby cars honked at the couple, as if that was even remotely helpful. I tossed the wife a sympathy smile as I ran by, but I was secretly hoping they stayed stuck for a while. As long as the road was blocked, no one could get in or out. I could only hope Jude was stuck in the traffic, as well.

People were lined up outside the Marina's main office, and the line was so long it ran out the door and around the back of the building. Several people yelled at me as I cut through the line, but I ignored them. It took a few seconds for my eyes to adjust to the gloom inside the office. Matthew had all of the shades drawn. The room was stagnant and warm. The smell of sweat and sand filled the small space.

I ran to the desk and cut in front of a burly woman wearing a t-shirt with a picture of a howling wolf on it. She was complaining that she should receive a refund on the inner tube she rented because it inexplicably popped while her son was riding it. Her son, equally burly and no more than ten-years-old, had a pocket knife clipped to the elastic waistband of his swimming trunks. Mystery solved.

"Watch it, lady," she said, raising her voice as I moved in front of her, but stepping back to let me through. She was the epitome of all bark, no bite.

Matthew looked haggard. Dark semi-circles were painted under his eyes in thick strokes, and he had gone so slack-jawed that I began to wonder whether I shouldn't look for a lobotomy scar.

"Have you seen my sister?" I asked, the words tumbling out of my mouth, tripping over one another.

Matthew started as if he had been sleeping with his eyes open, and then blinked once, focusing on my face. His eyes went wide. "Oh, thank God," he said, reaching across the laminate desk to grab my arm. "I've been trying to get in touch with Blaire all day."

Hope swelled in my chest. Did he know something about Page that he'd been trying to alert us to? Had he seen her?

"She won't take my calls. I know she's mad at me, but I need to explain," he said.

His words were like a needle to the hope filled balloon in my chest. Pop.

"Matthew, I'm not here to help you get Blaire back. I need to know if you've seen my sister."

He released my arm and shook his head, and his forehead furrowed in concern. "I saw her walk by when I went to close the blinds earlier, but I haven't seen her since."

It was my turn to grab his arm. I pulled him across the desk towards me and looked directly into his eyes. "Was she by herself or was she with someone?"

Matthew had been happy to see me, but I could see that emotion waning rather quickly. "Alone, headed for the docks."

"Where does Jude Lawton keep his boat?" I asked.

"Who?"

I didn't have time for this. I walked around the desk, ignoring Matthew's protests, and found a map of the docks pinned to a bulletin board hanging on the wall, each tiny rectangle along the dock labeled with a number and a letter, but no names. I moved to the file cabinet under the desk and pulled open the drawer I'd seen Matthew open a few hours before when I rented the boat I'd taken to the cave. The file folders were alphabetical, and I flipped to the 'L' file. Lawton was printed in big block letters on the third form.

"You can't look through the files," Matthew said as I pulled Jude's file. "No one is supposed to be behind the desk."

"Should we call someone?" the woman in the wolf shirt asked. "This can't be legal."

I tuned all of them out as I skimmed Jude's file. He had been docking his boat on the island for almost six months, but according to the file, he was two months behind on his fees. I filed that information away in the back of my mind, and scanned the page for his dock number. Written in tiny scrawl in the top corner was '6M'. Grabbing the map and Jude's file, I bolted around the desk, dodging Matthew's half-hearted attempt to stop me from stealing a customer's file, and ducked outside.

The gray sky had finally opened up in a heavy mist, and the boat show goers and regular Marina visitors were taking refuge under the small amount of protection provided by the Marina's awning and the surrounding trees. I, on the other hand, darted into the wet road and sprinted for the docks. According to the map, 6M was at the end of one of the furthest docks. As I ran, the mist steadily turning to rain and clouding my vision, I prayed Page was still at the Marina. More than that, I prayed Jude hadn't found her yet.

I tucked the papers against my chest as the rain pounded down around me. People were running past me headed towards the Marina, inner tubes and body boards held above their heads to protect them from the rain. Several of them shot me confused looks as I squinted into the storm, searching for Jude's boat.

By the time I made it to the end of dock 6, it was clear which boat was Jude's. It was the only boat missing from the dock. I ran to the empty space, and triple checked the map to be certain I'd gone to the right dock. I had. Page was gone.

I pulled out my phone to call her before I remembered she didn't take her cell phone with her when she left. Page was gone. And so was Jude's boat.

A hand landed on my shoulder and I screamed, turning and swinging with my free arm at whoever had grabbed me.

"Whoa, sorry. It's me. It's me," Mason said, raising his arms in surrender.

"Page is gone," I said, rain freely pouring down my face now.

"I know," Mason said.

I shielded my eyes with my hand, and tilted my head to the side. "What do you mean? How?"

"I asked some of the guys at the Marina if they'd seen your sister or Jude. They said they saw them leaving together fifteen minutes ago. Jude had his boat keys with him."

"They're out on the water?" I asked, turning towards the bay. Visibility was almost non-existent and the tide would be coming in any second. Following them would be incredibly dangerous.

"I got a boat for us," Mason said. "We can follow them."

Almost as a warning from Mother Nature, a strong wind roared through the bay, rocking the boats docked at the Marina.

"I can't ask you to go out there and risk your life for me," I said. "I'll go."

Mason looked at me as if I'd just told him I was planning to chase my sister on the back of a narwhal. He grabbed my hand and pulled me after him. "The boat is this way."

Clearly, there would be no arguing with him on this point. Despite the anxiety of not knowing if Page was safe and growing steadily colder and wetter, my heart swelled. Once again, Mason was putting himself in harm's way to protect me and my family.

Even though I'd told Mason he didn't need to go out on the water with me, I was immeasurably glad he'd decided to come. The rental boat he acquired was in considerably better shape than the one I'd had earlier in the day, but it was still small, and Mason knew how to navigate it around the swells to avoid a good deal of jostling.

"Where are we headed?" he asked.

I pointed in the general direction of the cave and told him which landmarks to look out for. He nodded, and then gave all of his attention to steering the small boat into the increasingly choppy waters.

"How did you manage to rent a boat?" I asked. Not only had the line outside the Marina been considerable, but the Marina had a policy about renting boats during a storm.

Mason cast a nervous glance back to me and then to the floor of the boat. "I kind of went behind the desk and stole a key."

I couldn't help it, I burst out laughing, throwing my head back and letting my laughter join the roar of the storm. Mason raised his eyebrows at me, no doubt thinking I'd finally lost it.

"I dug around behind the desk and found where Jude Lawton kept his boat," I explained. "After this, we will probably be banned from the Marina for life."

Mason smiled at me. "We are like a regular Bonnie and Clyde."

"A proper criminal couple," I added.

We smiled at one another, enjoying the sweet moment in the midst of our crazy reality. As my smile began to fade from my lips, I saw the outline of the cave begin to break through the mist.

CHAPTER 19

"There it is," I shouted, pointing through the rain towards the shore. The cave was a large, dark bullseye in the storm. A beacon helping us find our way. I could only hope my sister wasn't lying inside it the way Theodore had.

Mason followed my finger and nodded, doing his best to head straight for the shore despite the waves continuously knocking us off course.

As we neared the shore, we could see the small wooden dock jutting out into the water with a boat tossing next to it.

"Is that Jude's boat?" Mason asked.

I squinted away the water, but it was impossible to tell. Not only did I have a rather mediocre knowledge of boats, but I was fairly certain the rain had washed out one of my contacts. "It has to be," I said. "Who else would be out in this storm?"

Mason's shirt and jeans were thoroughly drenched, his

dark hair plastered across his forehead, and I could tell by the tense look on his face that he agreed with me. "What do we do when we reach shore?"

I'd been thinking the same thing, but I still had no plan. We'd run out of the house so quickly that we hadn't thought to grab any weapons. I searched the bottom of the boat and found a broken fishing pole, some rope, and an empty metal tackle box. "I guess we'll figure that out when we get there," I said.

We pulled up to the dock opposite Jude's boat and I was scrambling out of our boat and onto the wood before Mason could even kill the engine. Jude's boat was empty, which was a relief. Images of Page tied up in the bottom of it had filled my mind the entire time we were crossing the bay. However, not seeing her created an entirely new anxiety. Where had Jude taken her?

Mason threw a rope around the dock and secured our rental before following me out and onto the sand.

"We have to be careful," Mason said. "If they're nearby, they definitely heard us arrive. I should have killed the engine further out so we could have snuck up on them."

"It's fine, Mason. If you had killed the engine, I would have jumped out and swam," I admitted. "I needed to get here as soon as possible."

The sand was thick and wet like cement, and it tried to suck my shoes off with every step. I looked behind me and watched as our footprints filled in with water, the sand clamoring to fill the holes as quickly as possible. If Jude and Page had walked through here, it would be hard to tell now.

"Do you see anything?" Mason asked.

I shook my head. "The rain is erasing their tracks."

A scream broke through the storm, a high-pitched whine amidst the low rumbles of thunder, and the hair on my arms stood up.

"Page!" I screamed back, twisting my head from side to side, looking up and down the beach. I'd recognized her voice, but I couldn't pinpoint where it had come from.

I sprinted straight ahead towards the cave, throwing caution to the wayside. Mason shouted after me, and then I heard his heavy breathing as he followed me.

The ground levelled out as I ran, the sand growing thinner until I was standing on a large stone surface at the mouth of the cave. Even in the gloom brought on by the dark storm clouds, I could see the back wall of the cave. It looked much as it had a few hours earlier, only much wetter. Rain had drifted in on the wind, leaving muddy puddles in the low spots of the cave floor.

"Page!" I screamed again, though it was clear she wasn't in the cave.

"I couldn't tell where the scream came from," Mason said. "Are you sure it's Page?"

"Positive," I said, nodding my head emphatically, though I wished more than anything there could be even a shred of doubt. I didn't want to believe my sister was in serious danger. As I turned to leave the cave, a glimmer caught my eye. I dropped to my knees and crawled towards the edge of the cave. Lying half submerged in a puddle was the mermaid.

I picked it up and held it out to Mason, my eyes wide. "Page had this when she left the house today."

Mason tightened his lips into a straight line just as

another scream crashed around us. Inside the cave, the noise sounded impossibly far away.

I groaned in frustration, throwing the mermaid at the cave wall, where it hit with a sickening metal crunch and bounced to the floor.

Mason grabbed my arm and pulled me out of the relative safety of the cave and back onto the sand. The storm was raging in full force—lightning flashing across the sky in a near-continuous light show, thunder rumbling low and loud like a drumroll.

He let go of my hand long enough to clench and unclench his fists, then he turned to me, grabbing me by the shoulders. "I'm going to sound like the guy who plays Body #1 in a horror movie, but we have to split up."

I bit my lip and glanced around, hoping to see a large arrow pointing to where Page was being held. When that failed to materialize, I nodded in agreement. "You head east, I'll head west. Shout if you find something. If neither of us finds anything," I paused, praying that wouldn't be the case. I had to find Page. Failure was not an option. I took a deep breath. "If neither of us find anything, we meet on the back side of the island and then walk back here together, so we can go to the mainland and get the police."

"Did I not mention that?" Mason asked. "I called Shep right after I stole the boat."

I threw myself at Mason, wrapping my arms around his neck and kissing him. It was a quick kiss, but it was enough for warmth to spread in my arms and legs. I pulled back to look at him. His lips were still puckered, his eyes wide with surprise. "Shout if you find something. If not, I'll see you on the other side."

He gave me the smallest smile and nodded. "See you on the other side."

The island was quite small, completely empty of any manmade structures aside from the dock, but it felt enormous as Mason and I moved in opposite directions. I turned around several times as I followed the curve of the beach, watching as he grew smaller and smaller, and then, finally, disappeared around the curve. Palm trees dotted the shore and turned to a thick forest in the center of the island. Small caves worn smooth by the water from high tide popped up occasionally, as well.

I was nearing the western edge of the island, my legs tired and heavy from trudging through the soggy sand, when another scream erupted, this one closer than any of the others. It felt as though I'd been hit with a bolt of electricity. My fatigue disappeared, replaced by pure adrenaline.

"Page!" I screamed, running further down the beach, following the sound of her scream.

"Piper!"

My heart soared. I'd found her, and she was alive. As long as I could hear her screaming, Page was alive.

Another cave was visible just over a hill and to the left. It sat in the lowest part of the island, and the shoreline was creeping up towards it. The trees near the cave showed water lines several feet off the ground, and I knew we only had fifteen minutes, at most, before the tide came in and the whole stretch of beach would be entirely under water.

"Where are you?" I called, still moving towards the cave. I just needed to know Page was okay. I needed to hear her voice again.

No response.

"Page, where are you?" I asked again, my jog quickly transitioning into an all-out sprint, my heart rate ratcheting up until I thought it would burst.

Still no response.

Tears stung the corners of my eyes, but I held them back. I didn't have time to cry or worry. I had to find my sister.

As I neared the cave, water splashed around my ankles, inching higher with every step. The cave was surprisingly small once I was up close, the ceiling only a foot taller than me, the mouth of it no more than ten-feet wide. It went deeper than the other cave, though, and the back wall was hidden in shadows.

"Page!" My voice echoed off the stone walls.

Suddenly, a flash of movement in the center of the cave floor caught my attention. A pale hand sticking up from the floor waved from side to side. Page. I was so ecstatic to see her that I didn't catch the words she kept repeating until it was too late.

"Watch out."

Immediately, something grabbed the hair at the back of my head and pulled me out of the cave and back into the rain. My feet slid out from underneath me and one of my sandals slipped off and was pulled into the cave by the tide.

I opened my mouth to scream for Mason in case he hadn't heard me yelling for Page, but a warm hand clamped over my mouth and nose, stealing my breath. I struggled, kicking out with my bare foot and flapping my elbows, but I couldn't land any hits.

"Stop struggling," a familiar voice hissed in my ear. "You're only making this harder on yourself."

Even as he was threatening me, I couldn't help but imagine Jude doing the voice over for a car commercial on television or hosting his own radio show where he gave love advice to desperate women. His voice was syrupy sweet and smooth, adding a surreal layer to the situation.

In what little light was offered by the dark gray sky, I could see Page moving weakly in the back of the cave, flinching away from the approaching water as the tide rose. I wanted to shout at her to move, to run while Jude was distracted, but I could barely breathe around Jude's hand. As he dragged me further from the cave, a break in the clouds allowed a ray of sunshine to drop onto the beach, and I saw why Page wasn't running. She'd been tied down.

Thick ropes held her arms to her sides and bound her ankles together. She wriggled against her bindings, but to no avail.

Jude dropped me hard in the sand, my back landing on a protruding rock. I scrambled quickly to stand up, but his foot landed on my chest and pinned me to the ground.

A mask of anger wrinkled his brow and turned his kind smile into a grimace. "You might as well lay back and enjoy the show," he said.

I grabbed at his foot, trying my best to lift it from my sternum if only so I could fill my lungs with fresh air.

"I'd bet we have ten minutes before the tide is full in. What do you think?" he asked, grinding his foot harder into my chest. "Though, your sister will be swallowing water long before then. I'd give her six minutes. Care to make a friendly wager?"

CHAPTER 20

Jude was going to let Page drown.

A pit yawned open in my stomach, consuming me until I could no longer feel my own body lying in the sand. I couldn't feel the soft rain peppering my cheeks or the rock lodged beside my spine. All I could feel was an achy emptiness where my stomach should be.

"You're sick," I said, scratching at the annoyingly thick fabric of Jude's jeans, using what remained of my strength to try and pry his foot off of me.

He laughed and pushed down harder. Wet sand crept up over my arms and legs, threatening to swallow me whole. It felt as though I'd been encased in cement.

"Under different circumstances, me and your sister would have really hit it off," he said, smiling as he looked up towards the quickly disappearing clouds, blue sky peeking through the gray. "And I'm sure the two of us would have been thick as thieves. I would have made a nice addition to the family."

Was this guy insane? He had known Page for a few days, and he was talking about being part of the family *while* waiting for Page to die?

"We make it a rule not to marry murderers," I spat.

"A murderer," Jude said, testing the word out on his tongue. "I suppose I am a murderer now. I never thought that would happen. I only came here to sell a boat."

"I hate to break it to you," I said, "but you can't sell a boat to a dead man."

He laughed. "You also can't sell a boat to a man who has no money."

I wanted to ask what he meant, but at that moment he shifted his weight onto me, practically crushing my rib cage, and I was too busy gasping for air to probe deeper into his motive. Fortunately, Jude decided to continue unprompted.

"As I'm sure you've already put together, the dead guy was supposed to be my buyer, but he showed up to the exchange with no money. And things became a little heated. I may or may not have shoved him, and he may or may not have busted his skull open on a rock."

Jude admitted to murder as casually as if he was admitting to eating the last slice of cheesecake.

"Why not just find a new buyer?" I wheezed.

Jude looked down at me, a question written in the lines of his forehead, as if he couldn't figure out why I was so short of breath, but he didn't bother removing his foot from my midsection. "I would have, but there was no more time. Debt collectors wait for no one, and I quite like my legs unbroken, thank you very much. So, once I realized he was dead, I grabbed his wallet. Luckily, he had enough cash in there to buy me a few more days, but not enough to pay for my room at the bed and breakfast. Sorry about that," he said, wincing.

"All is forgiven," I said, launching into another attack on his leg, trying to garner enough momentum to lift myself out of the sand.

"I was planning to sell my boat and quietly slip away, but then someone found the body and I had to stay and divert attention from myself," he said. "Believe it or not, I really did like Page, so I hated doing it to her, but she was the easiest choice. I made some anonymous tips to the police station, invited her onto my boat so I could claim she killed Theodore and used my boat without my knowledge—though your island's laughable police force never even got that far—and planted the wallet in her room. It was almost too easy. But then—"

"Yeah, yeah, I know the spiel," I said. *"If it hadn't been for you meddling kids."*

Jude laughed. "See? This is what I mean. You and I would have become great friends, I'm sure. Ah well," he said wistfully.

I rolled my head to the side and looked back over towards the cave. I could still see Page, though the tide had risen high enough that she was now straining to keep her head out of the water.

Jude followed my gaze. "It won't be long now. What did I say it would be? Six minutes?" he looked down at his watch. "Ahh, it's only been three minutes. I may have overshot by a minute or two. That's exactly what got me into this problem in the first place," he said, bending forward to fold his arms over his knee, putting even more weight onto my body. "I should really give up gambling."

Gambling?

Theodore was dead because of Jude's gambling debts? Page and I were minutes away from death because Jude couldn't quit gambling while he was ahead? If I hadn't been pinned to the ground, I would have hurled myself at Jude. Perhaps even smashed a rock over his head. Seen how he liked it.

As it was, I couldn't move so I rolled my head in the opposite direction, trying to get my anger under control so I could think of a plan. I needed a clear head. That was when I saw a flutter of movement in the trees along the beach.

Mason. He was crouched low, moving down the beach towards us. He must have heard me calling for Page before Jude attacked me. I felt like I could finally breathe. Despite Jude's crushing weight on my chest and the wet sand pressing in on me, I felt light as a feather. We were going to be okay. We were all going to get out of this alive. Mason caught my eye and motioned for me to keep Jude talking.

"Why haven't you thrown me in the cave with Page?" I asked. "Why not kill us both at the same time?"

"I don't have enough rope," he shrugged. "Besides, you'd almost certainly find your way out of the ties and save yourself and your sister. It's better if I kill you separately."

"How are you going to kill me?" I asked.

Jude smiled. "I'm so glad you asked. Maybe I can get your help with this because I can't make up my mind."

I chanced a look over at Mason. He was directly behind Jude now, creeping out of the dense trees as quietly as he could, a large rock held in his hands.

"I was thinking I could untie Page once she succumbs to the water, and use the same rope to string you from the tree. Something about that seems poetic, don't you think? However, I could also make it easy on myself and just do away with you the same way I did Theodore. Find a large rock and just—"

Jude brought his arms over his head at the same time Mason lifted the rock above his head. As Jude's arms swung downward, Mason smashed the rock into the back of Jude's head.

It was almost comical, the look of confusion that flashed across Jude's face in the moment before he fell forward. He stumbled off of me, and I took a deep breath, finally filling my lungs. Mason jumped over me, bringing the rock down on Jude again as he attempted to crawl away.

I heard the crunch of bone, but I didn't stay to see the outcome. I scrambled to my feet and ran towards the cave.

Page's face was half-submerged in the water, only part of her mouth and nose sticking out. Her eyes were wide and panicked.

I splashed to my knees in front of Page and lifted her out of the water, pulling her into my chest. I wrapped my arms around her and stroked her wet hair. The moment we touched her face crumbled into a sob, her shoulders shaking with unspent emotion.

"You're okay," I whispered, both to her and to myself. My heart was pounding so hard I thought it would break my ribs. "You're going to be okay."

EPILOGUE

"Can you tell your stalker to take a hike? He's scaring away the guests." Page ruffled Blaire's hair as she dropped a plate of pancakes in front of her.

Blaire drowned the plate in syrup and shrugged. "I can't help it that he's obsessed with me. Once you go Blaire, you don't go back."

She waggled her eyebrows at me, sticking her tongue out between her teeth, and I pretended to gag myself with my finger.

"You need to either forgive him or let that boy go before he becomes a permanent lawn ornament," I said. "The lawn guy actually asked me yesterday whether he should ask Matthew to move or mow around him. It's becoming a problem."

Blaire smiled, clearly enjoying Matthew's groveling. "There's no rush. I don't want to take him back if he isn't truly sorry, and I won't know if he's truly sorry until he has spent at least two consecutive months standing outside my bedroom window."

Then, her eyes lit up. "Hey! That's what the psychic must have meant! She told me not to rush!"

"Don't tell me we're still talking about that psychic," I said. "She was such a fraud!"

"Cibil is not a fraud!" Blaire shouted, her mouth held open as if I'd insulted her to her very core. "She got both of our predictions right."

I groaned.

"Groan all you want, Aunt Piper, but she pegged you, too. She said there was violence in your future."

Page perked up. "What's this about violence and psychics?"

"Nothing," I said, glaring at Blaire.

Page had been a touch on the sensitive side since her encounter with Jude. It didn't matter that Mason had killed Jude on the scene, and Page had been fully exonerated of Theodore's murder. Page still had nightmares about Jude most nights, and she had firmly shut down the idea of going on any more dates for the foreseeable future. The last thing we needed to do was bring him up at the breakfast table.

"Yeah, nothing," Blaire said, focusing very intently on her pancakes. Though I saw her throw me one last knowing look, trying to convince me of Cibil's validity, before she dropped the subject for good.

Even though Cibil's prediction had *technically* been right, I didn't believe she could see into the future. In reality, she had probably seen my face in some of the local papers in connection with the murderous party at Robert

Baines' house and given me a vaguely violent prediction. However, if somehow she was actually a legitimate psychic, I had to wonder whether the encounter with Jude had been the extent of it. Would my life on Sunrise Island finally ease into the life of sunshine and beaches I'd imagined, or was more death and violence in my future? If I wanted to continue on with my life, I had to believe the worst was over. I had to believe life would normalize.

"No way!" Page shouted, her fork clattering to the table next to her.

Blaire and I both jumped at the sudden commotion, looking around for whatever had caused her outburst.

"What?" I asked, my heart racing.

"Do you hear that?" Page asked, her head cocked to the side.

Blaire and I both got quiet, listening. Finally, I heard it. The faint sound of a love song floating through the house.

"I think Matthew is playing music on the front lawn," Page said, clapping her hands in delight. "He pulled out a boom box for Blaire!"

Blaire groaned. "Okay, that is too much even for me. I've got to tell him to get lost."

Page and I couldn't hear her, though, because we were too busy belting out the second verse to "Forever Love."

Find out what mysteries lie ahead for Piper in Book 4, *A Secret By The Sea*.

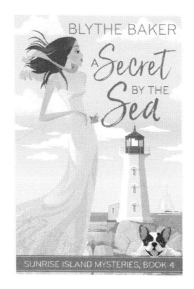

ABOUT THE AUTHOR

Blythe Baker is a thirty-something bottle redhead from the South Central part of the country. When she's not slinging words and creating new worlds and characters, she's acting as chauffeur to her children and head groomer to her household of beloved pets.

Blythe enjoys long walks with her dog on sweaty days, grubbing in her flower garden, cooking, and ruthlessly de-cluttering her overcrowded home. She also likes binge-watching mystery shows on TV and burying herself in books about murder.

To learn more about Blythe, visit her website and sign up for her newsletter at www.blythebaker.com

46804652R00123